BIBLIOGRAPHY

Psychological Thriller

Corvo Hollows

Alexa Bentley Paranormal Mysteries

Book One – Missing in Michigan
Book Two – Frightened in France
Book Three – Lost in Louisiana

Midnight Myths and Fairy Tales Series

Book One – Vasilisa the Terrible: A Baba Yaga Story
Book Two – Death Song of the Sea: A Celtic Story

Horror

The Haunting of Cabin Green: A Modern Gothic Horror Novel

REVIEWS

The Haunting of Cabin Green

"A spectacular read...absolutely gripping. I couldn't force myself to put it down. Taylor did an excellent and meticulous job creating this story, forming imagery...invoking real emotion on the part of the reader."
- *The Horror Report*

"April A. Taylor's *The Haunting of Cabin Green* sucked me in from the first page...Taylor pulls the rug out from under her readers...a well-structured and integrated climax. I read this book in one sitting...fighting the urge to turn on all the lights." - *Connal Bain, Author of Blood Moon Fever*

"Unique...the author depicts the grieving process amazingly well. The story is claustrophobic...and what an ending. All of the flashbacks and delusions suddenly make sense...[It's a] sucker punch." - *Jennifer Turner, HorrorTalk.com*

"A haunting tale." - *PopSugar*

THE
HAUNTING OF
CABIN GREEN

A Modern Gothic Horror Novel

April A. Taylor

Cover designed by OliviaProDesigns

This book is a work of fiction. Names, characters, places, and incidents either are products of the author's imagination or are used fictitiously. Any resemblance to actual persons, living or dead, events, or locales is entirely coincidental.

April A. Taylor
Visit my website at www.AprilATaylor.net

Printed in the United States of America

First Printing: April 2018
Midnight Grasshopper Books

Alexa Bentley Paranormal Mysteries

"Alexa (Alex) Bentley is the type of main character I love...the plot grabbed me and made me want to read on, while the lightheartedness made the story even more enjoyable...I couldn't work out the solution to the mystery...this is a book I would be quite happy to read a second time." - *Long and Short Reviews*

"The story is fast-paced, the plot entertaining, the characters - in particular Alexa - are intriguing... this is a gripping read that fans of paranormal mysteries will certainly enjoy." - *I Heart Reading*

"This is the best mystery/paranormal story I have read in a long time. It had great characters. It was filled with action and mystery. It kept me genuinely enthralled from beginning to end. Oh, and that ending!!! I can't wait to read the next Alexa mystery. I'm sure it's going to be another wild ride!" – *Boundless Book Reviews*

Midnight Myths and Fairy Tales

"Beautifully bewitching...it's a fast-paced, captivating tale, and the writing is exquisite." – *Amazon Reviewer*

"I was enthralled...The story is like a witch's spell drawing the reader in." – *Amazon Reviewer*

This book is for Anne and for every person who loves Gothic horror.

CHAPTER ONE

Ben's beloved Honda Civic cut through the thick, low-lying fog of a Michigan autumn night. Lost in thought, he didn't spot the person darting into the road until the last possible second. With a gasp, he slammed his foot onto the brake pedal, and all his fingers grabbed the steering wheel with authority for the first time that day.

His tires screeched against the pavement as he yanked the car around to avoid a collision. The blue Honda spun in a complete circle three times before stopping at a haphazard angle on the road's left shoulder. He put the car in park and reeled from the intense pounding of his heart.

Unsure what to do, he reflexively brought a cigarette butt up to his lips. It was burned down to sheer ash, and he took a drag of nothing but air. He didn't notice the lack of nicotine as a long trail of ashes sprinkled across his legs.

He wiped the sweat from his forehead and took a moment to collect himself. Ben was almost positive he hadn't hit anyone, but where had that person gone?

The reflection of his headlights off the wall of fog almost blinded him, so his lone option was to get out and search the immediate area. After rubbing the harsh, fog-induced white spots from his eyes, his awkward, lanky frame stepped free of the car. The long since extinguished cigarette butt slipped unnoticed from his fingers.

"Hello? Are you okay?"

The distorted chirping of hundreds of unseen crickets singing their nighttime song was the only response.

"I'm sorry if I scared you. Do you need help?"

His pulse sped up as he wondered if he'd hit the person without realizing it. This fear took root, growing and spilling out of him at a rapid pace. Frantic, he searched the road around him, but there was no sign of anyone.

Each uneventful second helped his trepidation subside, and he started to think his imagination was to blame. He hadn't slept well in months and had also been thinking about Kyra. Maybe it was natural to invent a ghost or two.

He resumed his search through the moist, oppressive air, but only to definitively confirm his hunch that he'd imagined the entire thing. The fog made the process difficult, but a full five minutes passed with no sign of anyone or anything. As he gave up and headed back toward his car, something connected with his shins and sent him flailing to his knees.

"Shit!"

His teeth chattered and his long, thin fingers trembled as he steeled himself to investigate the obstacle in his path.

Please don't be a body, please don't be a body...

Ben crawled toward his unseen assailant, half-convinced a hook-handed killer was lying in wait. His guts would soon be ripped asunder and his blood would redecorate the highway.

After ninety-three days of soul-shattering grief, he was stunned to discover the thought of dying under a madman's hook made him scared for his life. If someone had proposed this exact scenario to him yesterday, he might have asked, "Where can I sign up?" Unsure what the vast blanket of fog was hiding but certain he wanted to live, Ben's limbs stopped moving.

This is crazy. I know I didn't hit anything.

Another part of his mind refuted this logic.

Then why am I crawling in the middle of a highway?

As distasteful and terrifying as it was, he'd never be able to live with himself if he didn't uncover the identity of the object – *not a person* – that had tripped him. Hesitation clawed at every fiber of his being, but he forced his way forward until his right hand brushed a raw, rough surface. He yanked his hand back like it was on fire before regaining control of his actions.

I can do this.

Ben reached out again, and his fingertips came into tentative contact with the alien object. The moisture in the air hadn't seeped into its skin. His left fist covered his mouth to stop audible proof of his fear from escaping. At the same time, he increased the pressure of his right fingers in a bid to figure out what – or who – had gotten in his way. A crumbling sensation sent shock waves throughout his body. He managed to hold on long enough for a small sliver of something unknown to drop into his palm.

Unable to keep his composure any longer, he darted back to the car, careful not to drop the evidence. He slammed the door shut and jammed the locks in place before turning to face the source of his inevitable doom. With his eyes squeezed shut, he uncurled his fist and put the object on display. His left eyelid lifted a fraction of an inch to test the waters before he dove in and allowed both eyes to confront the truth.

A piece of old bark stared back at him.

A tree? It was a goddamn tree?

Ben understood then; there had never been a person darting across the road. Instead, the combination of fog and headlights must have somehow shot a reflection up into his view. If he hadn't been shocked enough to slam the brakes, he would have driven right into the fallen tree.

Grateful for this unexpected turn of events, he righted the angle of the vehicle and inched up the side of the road for an eighth of a mile to ensure he didn't have any other issues. He attempted to forget the incident, but his body was still soaked in sweat. A faint whooshing echoed from the tires as they reconnected with the grooves in the old country blacktop road.

The fog trailed behind his vehicle, lifting away from the fallen tree. He was sobered by the realization that his exhaustion and perpetual state of mourning could have killed someone. If Ben had done what he'd promised his friends, he wouldn't have been in this same area of the country, let alone on a deserted road late at night.

His hollowed out, pale green eyes shot up to the rearview mirror, but despite his recent scare, he still didn't see them or anything else the mirror had to show. In fact, he'd failed to notice almost everything during the past three months. That was the reason his friends had suggested taking a relaxing respite at a resort.

He'd agreed at the time that a temporary change of location might help him begin to deal with his grief, but he adamantly refused to let anyone go with him. Ben had begun to doubt this decision almost immediately after getting into his car, yet he hadn't reached out to anyone.

Continuing to drive up the old two-lane highway, Ben lowered the driver's side window in an attempt to rid his body of the stench of terror sweat. There was a slight crispness to the breeze, and the distinct redolence of autumn launched an attack on his olfactory system.

This was once a magical time of year; he and Kyra had met at a Halloween party. People can debate the existence of love at first sight all they want, but for the two of them, it was instantaneous.

After their introduction, they moved on to a real conversation rather than parting with the typical pleasantries. Several hours later, they were both surprised to learn the party was coming to an end. Neither had spoken more than a couple of words to anyone else, and they had sat together for hours in front of the fire pit.

The aroma of burning leaves was forever etched in his memory with her and, unsurprisingly, it had become a scent he adored above most others. Encountering it now was gut-wrenching, and yet still comforting, too.

While his thoughts lingered around the unique essence of fall, his foot resumed its former pressure upon the gas pedal, pushing the car to a speed it was almost uncomfortable with. The effects of the near possible accident were wearing off, and the ever-present numbness had returned with reinforcements.

Ben was no longer sure why he had agreed to make this trip.

Wouldn't it have been easier to keep sequestering myself at home?

Doubts swirled in his head as he made the final turn into the woods that would lead him to the cabin he'd dubbed 'Cabin Green.' Branches, leaves, and rocks crunched underneath his tires as the stereotypical owl from countless Halloween stories hooted to deride his arrival.

Wildlife was more abundant in these woods than in any other place he'd ever visited. The various year-long inhabitants only begrudgingly shared the property with him and his friends, and he'd often perceived the birds and animals as sneering at them.

The cabin came into view, and Ben was shocked by how dilapidated it looked. What he'd once viewed as rustic charm now looked uninviting and sad. He had the urge to turn around and flee but reminded himself it was a six-hour drive to get back home.

As he pulled the lone bag out of his car, he discovered the cabin's issues went much further than basic dilapidation; the exterior was cold and foreboding. It had been a warm place filled with lots of laughs and great times for several years, but the memories of those events had left the area. The cabin almost seemed evil now, but when he allowed that word to flit across his mind, he felt ridiculous.

"There is no such thing as an evil building," Ben chided himself, but he still hesitated at the base of the short staircase up to the front door. After a couple of seconds, he shook his head back and forth a few times, trying to dislodge the unwelcome thoughts from his mind.

"This is silly."

He had spent several happy, uneventful weeks here in the past. He decided he was simply experiencing the after-effects of what had happened on the road earlier, and he had to admit it still had him a little spooked.

That had nothing to do with this cabin and everything to do with a lack of sleep.

After struggling with the unfounded notion of evil for a few beats longer, he walked up the steps, opened the screen door, and slid his old, rusted skeleton key into the key hole. As he turned the key to the right, the locking mechanism made an audible click and the door creaked open.

Ben paused before he stepped across the threshold. It wasn't until he was in the cabin that he realized he was holding his breath like he did while swimming underwater. With a sharp exhale, air pushed past his quivering lips as his hand reached around in the darkness for a light switch.

A split second stretched into hours within his feverish imagination before the cabin came to life under the slight glow of a sixty-watt light bulb. The combination of dark wood and furniture made lighting a real challenge and would have muted even the brightest of bulbs.

His bag dropped to the floor as he took in his surroundings. To some, the natural dankness of the cabin might not seem welcoming, but Ben had spent so much time here that he knew the darkness wasn't hiding anything malevolent. He quickly became embarrassed by his initial irrational gut reaction. With a forced laugh, he resolutely went about the tasks of moving past it and getting unpacked.

Walking into the tiny bedroom brought memories of Kyra to the forefront of his mind. Her fresh, light perfume tickled his nostrils before disappearing entirely. Instead of dumping the scant contents of his bag into the dresser, he stumbled to the edge of the bed and sat down. His stomach and chest clenched with pain, and his tears fell with the intensity of a summer thunderstorm.

Without realizing it, he climbed further onto the bed and curled up into a ball. The musty, faded red bed sheet underneath him was soaked through to the mattress by the time sleep granted him a much-needed reprieve.

CHAPTER TWO

His arms encircled her, pulling her close to his bare chest. Her intoxicating perfume wafted around him, leaving him with the pleasant headiness of a stiff alcoholic beverage. Her lithe frame fit against his in a way that no other person ever had. Ben smiled for the first time in weeks and hoped the moment would never end.

His eyes squeezed together with no light penetrating them. "I love you," he murmured while kissing the nape of her neck. She didn't respond.

"Kyra?" he said, with more insistence than his last words. Still, she didn't respond, despite her breathing pattern making it clear she wasn't asleep. Furrowing his brow in confusion, he wondered why she wasn't answering him.

"Are you awake, hon?"

The stillness around them was maddening. He opened his eyes out of frustration, breaking the peaceful spell that the darkness had held on him. She wasn't there.

"Kyra?"

A slight panic set in as he reached out to feel around the bed. His hands examined the coarse bed sheet but found nothing else there.

"Kyra?"

He sat up, drenched in sweat. Ben remembered that Kyra wasn't here and would never be here again. Despondent, he laid his head down upon the pillows that had always been too firm for his tastes.

I don't understand. I could feel her, she was right here.

As they had a few hours before, tears wracked his body until he fell back asleep.

Several hours later, a ray of light drifted across the bed, warming his legs and chest before making it to his face. With a slight groan, he realized it would be futile to try to keep sleeping, so he allowed his eyes to open. The sunlight hit them like an invasion, and he hastily covered them with his forearm.

Is the sun brighter in the north?

Before the cabin clock's second hand made a full revolution, he gave up and consented to enter the waking world by re-opening his eyes. This time, they didn't recoil, but he did see little dark spots swirling in the air. Ben was shocked to discover he'd gotten a full night's sleep. This was the first time he'd stayed asleep for more than an hour at a time since the accident.

Somehow, his rested limbs were still heavier than lead and fog swirled inside his head. He was also vaguely unsettled, like there was something important he couldn't quite remember. Attempting to wrest this thought from his memory, he placed his bare feet on the wooden floor and shuffled off into the kitchen with nothing else but coffee on his mind.

"Fuck!"

The coffee maker refused to cooperate.

"What now?" he moaned while looking around for alternative options.

"Maybe it's just the plug," he said to no one in particular, followed by unplugging the vital appliance and carrying it to a distant outlet in the next room. Satisfaction filled his face as the coffee maker's clock lit up under the current of the secondary outlet.

Inhaling the aroma of the ground up beans, Ben scooped them into the filter and walked back into the kitchen to turn on the faucet. The pipes groaned in protest, but clear and fresh-smelling water soon gushed forth without any specific direction. The water splashed onto his arms and up into his face, and he let out a rare laugh at the unexpected shower.

Ben returned to the coffee maker, brimming with anticipation. Soon, the tantalizing fragrance of brewing coffee filled the small cabin. He poured himself a cup and walked into the enclosed patio. The view of the lake was astonishing as always, both in its beauty and simplicity.

A sense of awe swelled up inside of him, and he decided to explore further. Fortunately, a rock trail led down to a primitive dock over the water, and it had his name written all over it.

A slight breeze swirled around him as he sat on the edge of the dock, dangling his feet mere inches above the lake's surface. He pondered over dipping his toes in as he sipped at his coffee but remembered the water would be much colder than the mild, sun-drenched air around him.

Long gone were the days of ice forming on the lake by Halloween. Climate change had considerably altered Michigan's autumn season since then, and it was now often possible to sit by the lake during early October without needing to bundle up. Curious about how cold the water really was, Ben promised himself he'd find out later in the day.

A sense of peace and relaxation came over him. Its presence startled Ben because he'd grown so used to the negative fragments of thought that had consumed his mind for months. Grateful for the silence, he took another drink of his coffee before putting the mug down and lying back on the wooden dock. He allowed his eyes to close as he reveled in the sounds of nature.

* * * * *

Ben's eyes jerked open. The remnants of a noise he couldn't place fluttered through his ears. He waited for a moment as the normal sounds of nature overtook whatever he'd heard. Just as he began to think he'd imagined it, the sound returned.

"There," he said, as he turned around in time to see the patio screen door banging in the frame. Ben recognized this as what he'd heard the first time and felt silly for having been startled, especially on a windy day. He frowned at the distraction for a brief moment before choosing to ignore it.

All fear and anxiety melted away again as he closed his eyes while letting out a long, exaggerated yawn. Ben slipped back into a state of peaceful oblivion. His sleep was dreamless and long, and his eyes did not re-open until the sun had moved behind the cabin. When they finally did begin to flutter open, they were greeted by a peaceful blue sky.

A contented sigh escaped from his lips. After lying still for a little longer, he gave into the hunger that had awakened him. He'd had no interest in food for twelve weeks, and yet he now found himself craving scrambled eggs and toast.

Knowing there was nothing in the kitchen, he passed through the cabin, put on an old white t-shirt, and picked up his keys. He pulled the front door shut behind him, while simultaneously turning to lock it.

Ben stuck the key into the keyhole, but it did not turn. Instead, the door popped back open. Frowning, he yanked on the door with more force. After two more failed attempts, he succeeded at getting the lock to engage.

The drive to the closest gas station was short and uneventful. No one paid much attention to him, and he was able to purchase scant provisions without having to say more than two words to anyone. This suited him well and was a welcome break from the typical shopping experience.

He was disappointed to discover that his dream of eggs and toast was for naught, but he did find a tasty looking pre-made sandwich and some apples. As he loaded a single bag into the trunk, he mused over the simplicity of life in a place like this.

Would being here all the time make life more worthwhile?

While approaching the front door of the cabin, he remembered the difficulties he'd had locking it earlier and offered a silent prayer that he would not have any issues now. Ben's wish was granted as the skeleton key fit in and turned with ease. Walking across the threshold, a slight chill made his skin tingle, but he attributed it to the changing temperature that occurred at this time of day.

His stomach growled with such ferocity he could hear it, and this brought a hint of a laugh to his lips. It was a cliché to say country air makes things better, but perhaps it wasn't a lie, either. With great anticipation, he unwrapped the sandwich and took a big bite.

The unfounded thoughts that had entered his mind last night seemed even more ridiculous in the light of day. He was grateful for several hours of good sleep, a couple of near laughs, and actual hunger. All this combined to make him almost resemble a normal human being again. Ben wasn't cognizant of the events of late last night, and if anyone had asked him about it, he wouldn't have remembered anything.

Apple slices made a nice dessert and quieted his stomach's ravenous desire. While chomping on the last piece, he walked into the enclosed porch at the back of the cabin.

With a creak, the nineteen-seventies styled lime green chair accepted his weight. He leaned back as far as he could and looked up at the ceiling for a beat before pulling a pack of Marlboros out of his pocket. The first inhalation of smoke shocked his senses. He hadn't smoked since the night before and hadn't really tasted a cigarette in a long time. Somehow, it managed to taste both wonderful and terrible.

Smoke trailed off the end of the cigarette, and it caught a glint of light from the setting sun. Fascinated by the look of it, he took another puff.

Ben's memories transported him six years into the past, all the way back to his first visit to the cabin. His friend, Doug, had driven the two up north so Ben could decide whether or not to invest in what they were envisioning as a hunting cabin.

Upon seeing it for the first time, Ben said, "Yeah, this looks great; it reminds me a lot of a place my parents and I stayed on vacation once. This cabin green has lots of potential!"

"Cabin green?" Doug asked with a chuckle.

"Um, yeah, I mean green cabin."

Ben nervously pushed his black hair back. Inverting words was something he did every so often, just like everyone else. To his ears, though, it was a major catastrophe each time it happened, which left him with red cheeks and a sense of shame.

"Naw, man. You had it right the first time," Doug grinned.

With growing enthusiasm, the blond-haired, barrel-chested guy in his mid-twenties, once a local football hero, clapped Ben on the back.

"Cabin green. I like the sound of that. It's like an official title. I hereby christen you Cabin Green," he said to the cabin's front door while performing a comical looking routine with his hands.

Although his embarrassment about the accidental wordplay lingered for a while, the name Cabin Green had stuck. Doug reported the name, but not the incident behind it, to all their friends. Before long, everyone referred to it the same way.

Lost in thought, one cigarette turned into another until Ben finally snapped back into reality. Nauseated and lightheaded, he turned his back on the picturesque scene of the setting sun and went into the cabin. Without giving it any conscious thought, he disrobed, walked to the bathroom and turned on the shower with the hot knob twisted as far as it would go.

The small bathroom filled up with steam. The water woke his body from the stupor of the past three months; every pore on his flesh opened up wide and reveled in the accompanying sensations. He put his head underneath the near scalding water and allowed it to run through his hair and down his neck.

In a happy turn of events, there was some leftover soap and shampoo in the shower from his last visit to the cabin. In his haze of mourning, he hadn't thought to pack toiletries.

He recognized he only had enough supplies to stay clean for a couple of days. It was going to be necessary to make a trip to the local laundromat before everything ran out. There was a small part of him that tried to convince himself to do otherwise to minimize human interaction, but his body responded that the hot water and cleansing process felt much too good to be ignored.

Strange noises abruptly emanated from above Ben's head. At first, he thought they were coming from the water system, but he soon realized that wasn't the case. After pondering other likely possibilities, something disturbing came to mind - *there could be an animal trapped in the duct work.* Glancing up at the unfinished ceiling, he thought, *if there is an animal trapped there, I need to get out of the shower right now.*

Knowing an animal could fall on his head and doing something about it were different things. In fact, he tried to ignore this information, but the noises became louder and more erratic. Irked at the end of his enjoyable respite, he stepped out of the standalone shower and onto the dampened floor.

Ben pulled an old, miasmic towel off the rack and wrapped it around his waist as a wave of despair threatened to knock him to his knees. The temporary break the day had provided somehow made him even less capable of bearing up under the weight of what had become a typical emotion.

His eyes filled with tears and he stumbled through the cabin until reaching the small bed with the crumpled red bed sheets. He fell asleep with tears in his eyes for the ninety-fourth night in a row.

* * * * *

As the late-night stars twinkled, Ben woke up and found Kyra pressed against him. Although he didn't remember the previous night's events, he somehow understood he shouldn't open his eyes. Pressing them together as tightly as they'd go, he reached out his arms. She folded inside of them with no resistance, and her breath danced upon his naked chest.

He held her for several minutes before beginning to kiss her, first upon her cheeks and then her lips. The kisses were tentative and sweet, but once she returned his affection, Ben became more aggressive.

They were soon sharing the type of kisses most couples reserve for the short window between finding new love and settling into a routine. Before he could slip inside of her, she took matters into her own hands. Her touch set off a chain of events that left him happily exhausted.

He tried to fight the urge to snooze, but the need was much too strong. Ben floated into a deep, pleasant sleep with Kyra snuggled against his chest.

CHAPTER THREE

Dawn broke over his face for the second morning in a row, which elicited a groan while he tried to open his eyes. After several aborted attempts, he managed to get them open for long enough to see the mess he had made of his sheets. This woke him like a slap to the face because he didn't remember what happened, and it shocked him to see evidence of any type of sexual yearning.

Ben had been numb in that regard throughout everything and had been fine with that. Now, it seemed dirty and wrong to see he must have had an erotic dream. His stomach clenched with the violation of cheating on his fiancée, even though that was completely irrational.

* * * * *

Their wedding had been less than one week away when the accident took her from him. Ben felt betrayed by the world when she died, along with the God he had once believed in. Everything that had happened since then had been a blur of mourning; first, there was the wake he was too grief-stricken to remember, followed by sympathy cards and pan after pan of overcooked food he'd only picked at.

This initial outpouring of support came from almost everyone he'd ever met. However, the inherent impatience of humanity soon took over, and the majority of those early supporters had wandered off his path, perhaps never to return.

There was a small group of long-term friends who were still on his side, but even their attention to his constant need to rehash the past had recently been slipping. They might have had the best intentions when they suggested he take a relaxing vacation to get away from everything, but there was a festering part of his psyche that had become convinced their true motive was to get rid of him.

He hadn't admitted it to anyone else yet, but losing Kyra had left him disinterested in regaining any semblance of his former life. Then again, he hadn't told anyone much of anything since he began to see the glazed over look in their eyes. He had decided the old saying wasn't true; misery didn't love company. Misery only pushed others away.

* * * * *

Without pausing long enough to think, he ripped the sheets from the bed. A deep, skin-reddening shame compelled him to throw them away, even though he had access to a laundry facility not far from the cabin.

He walked barefooted down the narrow dirt path to the dumpster. His feet landed upon several rough spots, but he didn't notice, not even when part of a fallen branch scratched deeply enough into his skin to draw blood.

As he threw the sheets into the trash, an intense bout of stomach pain wracked his body so hard it caused him to double over. At the last possible second, his right hand reached out and grabbed the edge of the trash can to stop himself from falling.

A long, low moan radiated from his frame, and everything around him took on a hazy quality, as if he was looking at the world through beer goggles. Just as Ben began to believe the pain was going to pass, he vomited all over the ground below him, including on his own feet.

After becoming fairly certain he wasn't going to get sick again, he pulled himself back into a normal standing position and began assessing the situation. Clearly, taking a shower had become his first necessity. He returned down the same path and ascended the front entry steps, which each responded with a loud, startling creak.

That's odd.

In truth, those steps were always quite old, but they'd never been creaky or loose before. Out of the corner of his eye, Ben spotted some ivy making its way over the cabin's foundation. In his haste to get clean, these observations failed to make much of an impression. He entered the cabin and headed straight for the bathroom, so consumed with getting clean that he forgot to lock the door.

He turned the hot knob to full blast again and returned to the refreshing water that had given him so much peacefulness the evening before. That restorative quality didn't return, and he set about the task of cleaning himself as if he had undertaken a hated chore.

While scrubbing at his feet, he noted the same weird noises from overhead that had brought his last shower to a premature end. This time, he gritted it out and made sure to get himself as clean as possible before turning off the water. He stepped out of the shower and noticed there were no more towels in the bathroom. Irritated, naked, and dripping wet, he exited the bathroom and headed toward the bedroom.

As Ben rounded the corner from the kitchen, he spotted the reflection of a woman in the glass from the enclosed porch. Shocked, he dropped to his knees and attempted to cover himself while waiting for the inevitable scream that was sure to shatter the solitude of the cabin.

A few seconds later, the only sound he could hear was his heart beating in triple time. He cautiously rose into a near standing position. Holding still for a couple more beats, it sunk in that there were no signs or sounds of another person nearby.

Did I imagine her?

Despite his doubts, he still continued to guard his midsection while walking into the bedroom. The horrific, adrenaline-producing jolt of thinking that someone was there had turned the moisture on his body into sweat. He thought about taking a shower again but decided against it.

Before putting on his only other change of clothes, Ben used yesterday's towel to dry off. Still thinking about the weirdness of the past twenty-four hours, he got dressed and headed back out to the dock overlooking the water.

The wood creaked underneath him as he walked out to the farthest possible spot. Ben stood still and stared out at the water as an almost irresistible urge to dive in urged him to take action.

Indecision clouded his mind as he surveyed his surroundings. There was no one else around for miles, and he'd long since persuaded himself that the woman he thought he'd seen was nothing more than a stress-induced hallucination.

Choosing to abandon the confusion, Ben undressed down to his boxer shorts and leapt as far as he could. With a splash, his body cut through the icy cold water, and he put his time spent on the high school swim team to good use.

The water sparkled around him as he moved with fluid grace through the cleanest water he'd ever seen. His destination was a tiny island located less than a quarter of a mile from the shore. A school of small fish swam underneath him.

As always, getting dry land back under his feet felt almost alien at first. But then the warm rays of the sun fell upon him and he flopped down on his back, reveling in the warmth that had not broken through the surface of the water.

The island featured a short beach front, only extending back about five feet. He laid down upon the grass, with his feet touching the sand.

Lying there in the sunlight gave Ben a much-needed sense of safety and also made him nostalgic for better times. His mind meandered through its numerous pathways before landing on a particular memory.

* * * * *

Kyra was the most beautiful woman he had ever seen. Her radiance didn't come from so-called Hollywood good looks; rather, it came from a place far beyond the surface and broke through in her smile and dazzling hazel eyes.

He thought about their first real date, which fell on the Saturday after Halloween. Although they had connected at the party, he was clammy with nerves, much more so than he had ever been before any other date. He found out later she had felt the exact same way.

Ben had primped in front of the mirror for a good hour, rather than the typical five minutes, making sure his hair and cologne were perfect. He almost drove himself crazy changing his mind several times -*is this what women go through before a date?* – but eventually opted to wear a black button-up shirt and his dark blue boot cut jeans.

She was waiting in the lobby when he arrived at the little Italian restaurant she'd selected. Upon spotting him, her face lit up with a smile he would never be able to forget.

I'm going to marry this woman someday.

He made a mental note to temper down his enthusiasm so that he didn't come off as desperate or a freak. Just as he later found out she had been equally nervous that day, Kyra eventually confided in him that she'd also decided during their first date he was the man she wanted to marry.

He approached her, and the awkwardness melted away. They shared a quick embrace, and he kissed her dark olive cheek. Mere seconds later, the hostess told them that their table was ready, and he floated to his seat.

They didn't eat a lot of their pasta that night as the conversation flowed naturally from the moment they sat down. When the topic of religion came up, they dove right in rather than using any avoidance tactics.

"I was raised Hindu, and it was once a huge part of my life. But now? I don't know... I guess you could say I've been questioning my faith," she said as she reached out her hand and placed it on top of his.

"I can understand that," he replied. "My family was Baptist, but I've been agnostic for most of my life."

They left the restaurant three hours later, and he walked her to her car where they kissed for the first time before parting. After that date, they spent most of their time together. It happened organically, without any planning or discussion, and within two months they exchanged apartment keys.

Although they would stay overnight with each other an average of four nights a week, Kyra did not want to live together until they were married out of respect for her parents' deep-seated beliefs. He understood this, but because he was sure she was the one he wanted to be with, it also hastened his proposal time.

* * * * *

While reflecting on the past, he had been staring blankly in the direction of the cabin, not really seeing it, but still having it somewhat within his perception. His trip down memory lane was interrupted when a slight signal from his eyes trickled into his brain.

With a struggle, he forced himself to come back to the real world and peered across the water, shielding his vision from the brilliance of the sun. He searched around the perimeter of the house before settling on the thing that was out of place. There was smoke coming out of the ivy-covered chimney. That could only mean one of two things; a fire had been started in the fireplace or the cabin itself was on fire.

Without taking any time to consider the possibility that maybe he should stay far away from a fire and any strangers who might have come with it, Ben dove into the water and swam off at a speed that made his earlier trip look turtle-like. His body broke through the previously calm water, creating miniature waves.

The water was only a few degrees warmer than the last time, but his body became soaked with perspiration. The pounding of his heart filled his ears and lungs, and his limbs ached as he pushed himself harder toward the shore.

The smoke was getting thicker, billowing out in black clouds that began to settle and build a formation over the roof of the cabin. The charring of wood and something else that, although unidentifiable, seemed somehow very wrong, plagued his nose. This helped propel him even faster, despite the fear that gripped his mind.

Ben reached the dock and roughly pulled himself up onto it, breaking out into a run before becoming upright. The pungent smoke filled his nostrils as the heat of the fire danced upon his skin. His eyes stung as he ran up the steps of the back porch. His wet, bare feet were blasted by a violent, blistering heat as the water droplets clinging to them evaporated and turned into steam.

He became shockingly aware of the presence of fire on his skin and in his lungs as he ran into the center of the living room and looked quickly from side to side. He saw his beloved Cabin Green, and everything inside of it, turning to mere cinders and ash.

Ben fell to the scorching hot floor in agony. His skin caught fire, and the acrid smell of roasting human flesh wafted through the air. Screaming, he shut his eyes and put his hands over his ears while standing back up. An internal alarm sounded in his brain, which propelled him forward as he finally started running for safety. Three steps later, he tripped and fell headfirst into the fire.

* * * * *

"Oh, man," Ben weakly muttered upon regaining consciousness. A bolt of fear shot through his body, causing him to stand way too fast.

Hesitating, he opened one eye, then two. There was no fire in the fireplace, nor was there a fire anywhere to be seen.

He dashed through every room in the tiny cabin, and each one presented him with the same lack of anything different. The furniture wasn't scorched, let alone burned to ash. The walls weren't blackened by the insistent kiss of flames.

He still examined himself gingerly, expecting to see third-degree burns all over his body. As he thought about this expectation, it occurred to him that he wouldn't have had this level of mobility or presence of mind if he'd sustained severe burns. Still, it was a shock to discover that the vast majority of his skin had no marks at all. In fact, the only sign that something had happened was a minor and apparently unexplainable burn, no bigger than a penny, on his left hand.

"What the fuck?" Ben said as the rushing sounds in his ears settled down. Confused, he walked back outside the cabin and looked up into the sky. It was brilliantly blue. There wasn't a cloud of any sort as far as he could see.

As the adrenaline wore off, his body buckled under the full wrath of his frantic return journey. He fell to the ground in pain and fear. Was he losing his mind? Had it been a hallucination? Perhaps a trick of the light, somehow? But how had he felt the heat and smelt the smoke? How had it charred his lungs so much that his throat was still raw? How did his skin still insist it was afflicted with the lingering pain of multiple burns? Perhaps oddest of all, how did he end up with one small burn if he'd only imagined the fire?

CHAPTER FOUR

A frown engulfed Doug's face as he sat his iPhone down.

"It doesn't make any sense. Ben has never ignored my calls and texts before, and I got a 'read' receipt for each of my texts. I'm starting to get worried about him."

"I know, sweetie," a dark-skinned man in his early thirties with a chiseled face replied. "I also know the two of you have been practically attached at the hip since childhood, but he might need some time alone to finally process what happened."

Doug considered his husband's hypothesis. Ben *was* a sensitive guy, even more so than he liked to let anyone see. Maybe the effort of trying to deal with Kyra's death while everyone crowded around him was too much to bear.

"I guess that's possible," Doug said.

The more he thought about it, the less likely it seemed that Ben would completely cut him out, no matter what unspoken thoughts were darting about in his mind. The two had shared practically everything since they were ten years old. He had even turned to Ben first when he could no longer keep his sexuality a secret. Although they didn't have this aspect of their lives in common, Doug had always received genuine support from his friend, which became vital when he opted to keep the truth from everyone else until graduating from college.

Many people told Doug later on that they'd always suspected based on the fact that he was a good-looking, college football starter who'd never had a steady girlfriend. This irritated Ben, who'd also been without a steady girlfriend up until this point.

"Do they think I'm gay, too?" Ben asked.

Reading his friend's need to receive anything other than a pointless, halfhearted placation, Doug slipped into smartass mode. "Nah, they all thought you were just a weirdo. Which is less socially acceptable? Being gay or being a weirdo?"

For a split second, Ben looked like he was taking this comment seriously. Before Doug could begin to second guess himself, his friend's serious face turned into a mirthful one, and he laughed while replying, "I don't know, bro. We'll have to check this month's guide to being a social pariah."

The two cracked up inside of Doug's memory. It had always been like that between them. If Ben *had* been gay, the two would've almost certainly ended up together. Doug realized this long ago, but he was happier to have Ben as his best friend because that bond had stood the test of time.

Despite his strong belief that Ben would never ignore him, Doug had to acknowledge the fact that his friend had been through something extremely traumatic. It might be unrealistic to expect a quick reply during his respite period. Therefore, although he was still unsettled by the entire thing, he vowed to give Ben some space.

CHAPTER FIVE

Coming to terms with the idea that there was no way to know exactly what had happened that afternoon wasn't an easy feat, but Ben decided it was necessary to move forward. This involved numerous things, anchored most critically by his need for a trip into town. It was time to do laundry and pick up more food.

The point of his trip to the cabin wasn't to go even more insane; it was supposed to be a form of convalescence. Sitting in the cabin wondering about imaginary fires wasn't going to make him feel any better, nor was it going to give him any insight into how to move on from Kyra's death. On the other hand, doing everyday things such as laundry and shopping could help to reacclimate him to the world at large.

It had made sense when Ben was headed to Virginia Beach – as his friends had suggested - to pack a minimal amount of clothing because the resort featured full-service amenities, including free guest laundry. By coming to Cabin Green, he'd put himself in a position where it would become a bit of an issue if he didn't go into town every three days.

With a garbage bag containing his laundry securely placed inside the car, he searched the sky one more time for any possibility he'd missed some evidence there had actually been a fire. He saw nothing and climbed behind the wheel.

His Civic roared to life, and the engine noise echoed through the woods. He carelessly maneuvered it out of the gravel path and onto the real road that would lead to a form of civilization. He made note of the stunningly brilliant autumn leaves along the road; it was like being inside a Pure Michigan tourism advertisement.

The lone laundromat within a fifty-mile circumference was, fortunately, located only ten minutes from the cabin. He pulled up in front of it and noted with happiness that the recently remodeled Dash-n-Save next door was also open.

The door to the laundromat opened smoothly, accompanied by the jingle of a small bell. There was no one else around, but that didn't surprise him. Not only was the local population tiny but it was also a weekday at about three o'clock in the afternoon. Therefore, the locals were still working.

He had more than an hour and fifteen minutes to waste and nothing interesting to do during this time. Of course, he needed to do his shopping next door, but he didn't want to buy any food before the clothes were in the dryer. He was out of cigarettes, though, so he went next door anyway and purchased three packs of Marlboros.

Ben sat down at a wooden picnic table sitting on the property. While pulling the cellophane loose from the first pack of Marlboros, another smoker walked out of the little store and joined him at the table.

The man's face was crinkled with age, and he had the slightly protruding ear hair that Ben equated with elderly males. His steel blue eyes glinted in the sunlight, and although his frame was hunched forward, he was still massive. It wasn't that he was overweight; quite the opposite, in fact. He was strikingly tall and had a commanding presence, despite being almost scarecrow thin. When he sat down on the bench, it creaked and moaned with such severity that Ben was surprised it didn't break.

"Marlboro man, eh?" the man asked, with an approving tone. Without waiting for a response, he continued speaking. "I've been smoking for well on fifty some years now, and I've always been a Marlboro man myself."

They nodded at each other and placed the butt of their cigarettes between their lips in unison. The two men inhaled with their eyes closed before lifting their heads up toward the sky and exhaling with pleasure. They both noted the similarities and chuckled together.

"You're not from 'round here, are ya, fella?"

"No."

"What brings you this way, then?" The elderly smoker didn't ask this in a way that implied nosiness, more that he was simply trying to fill the silence.

"I'm staying at a cabin on the lake, about ten minutes from here."

The two men nodded at each other again and went on smoking in silence. Ben enjoyed the easy camaraderie with the older man. This simplistic back and forth, without any unnecessary male posturing, was what he'd wanted to have with his father.

Although he didn't know it, at least not on a conscious level, many of the tiniest details of Ben's life had been influenced by his early lack of a positive role model. Instead of having a supportive springboard that helped him deal with puberty while attempting to discover his true self, he'd had a toxic example of masculinity that left him afraid of his father and, at times, scared of becoming the same type of man.

Nothing about Ben had ever fit the image his dad desired. His father had solidified this thought by going out of his way to let Ben know that he looked at him as a huge disappointment. He wasn't strong enough, fast enough, or large enough, nor was he a lady's man, which often left his dad looking at him with disgust. He'd also "cried too damn much" as a child, which apparently meant he was a "sissy boy" and "worse than a damn woman." Reflecting upon his father's obvious scorn toward women made it clearer than ever why his parents' marriage had ended in disaster.

He'd continued to try to impress his father after reaching adulthood. Ben even picked up his nicotine habit from the man. He'd always believed his choice of cigarettes, Marlboro, was a solid, masculine option, but it hadn't pleased his dad. All he heard about for years after his dad discovered him smoking was that "real men don't need a damn filter."

In truth, there were only two things Ben had ever done that had pleased his father. The first was moving out. The second was going on an annual hunting trip. Of course, if his dad had ever found out the deer carcass photos Ben showed him weren't the result of his hunting prowess, there would have been a tremendous blowout. It might have even been worse than the day when the two of them found out Ben's grandfather, on his father's side, had left him his entire insurance policy.

The rage that emanated from his father that day was terrifying, but it also helped propel Ben toward a life far removed from his dad's presence. Looking back, he realized that might have been exactly what his grandfather had in mind.

The policy was enough to cover tuition at the University of Michigan, a modest condo, and all the wedding expenses. It had also helped him start a retirement fund and was now enabling him to take a much-needed sabbatical. Despite this influx of unexpected money, it was only Kyra's kind, nurturing presence that helped him begin to push past all his family-related baggage.

His father had passed away from lung cancer two years ago, and Ben was abashed to admit how much of a relief that had been. He'd tried a few times to give up smoking, but his old habit offered some comforting familiarity after Kyra's death.

The man stood, glanced at Ben, and said only "bye" in a friendly tone before walking away from the table. Encounters like this were typical in the area, but they never ceased to amaze those who didn't live here. It truly was a different place, even a different time.

While walking back inside the laundromat, Ben continued to reflect on the simplicity of living in a place where people weren't compelled to ask for your name.

How wonderful it could be to start over in a town like this. A place where no one would know his past and he wouldn't get those sideways glances people give when they're looking for signs of an upcoming mental collapse.

His thought patterns had been erratic and he'd vacillated daily, sometimes hourly, between the advantages of being here and not being here. But in this moment, Ben was glad he'd made the trip and wasn't in any hurry to leave.

His mind had compartmentalized the weird events of earlier after blaming them on a form of heat stroke, combined with a lack of food. After all, he'd been lying in the sun for a long time when it happened and also hadn't eaten anything yet that day. That combined with the exertion of swimming such a distance could surely cause anyone to hallucinate.

As to the woman he had thought he'd seen, well, she was also written off as a side effect of not having eaten anything. By the time he pulled his wet clothes out of the washer and tossed them into the dryer, he had decided to pick up enough food to last a week, along with some extra clothes so that he didn't have to frequently visit the laundromat.

Ben went back over to the store and picked up a little hand basket. His choices weren't exactly exciting, but he made the best of the few items the tiny, old-fashioned convenience store had in stock.

After adding two more packs of cigarettes to his order, he paid for everything with a credit card and headed outside. The sun was starting to go down, so he didn't worry too much about his items getting warm. Still, he placed them inside of the trunk because it would be the coolest possible spot.

Ben returned to the laundromat just as the dryer cycle ended. He smiled at the timing and pulled his warm clothes free of the dryer, audibly inhaling the fresh scent of a summer breeze. He placed the freshly folded clothing gently on the backseat. With a quick glance behind his car, he turned the engine and pulled out of the parking lot.

The roads were still empty when compared to Ann Arbor, but the four or five other cars fighting for tarmac space probably constituted a major local traffic jam. Ben rolled the windows down and enjoyed the crisp air as it swirled around inside of the car. Sooner than he would have thought possible, he found himself making the turn off into the woods.

Everything looked peaceful as he approached the cabin and, at first glance, he thought it was how he'd left it. However, upon closer inspection, there appeared to be a thicker concentration of ivy covering the chimney than he'd observed that morning.

The window frames had also accumulated a thin batch of ivy that he was certain had never been there before. Shrugging it off, he pulled the groceries from the car and walked up the steps of the porch. With a quick flick of his wrist, the door was unlocked and he walked in. Nothing but silence and normality greeted him, and he couldn't have been happier about it.

The bewildering events of the morning faded as Ben put his purchases away, then decided it was long past time to make some food. He pulled a frying pan out of the cupboard, tossed a small amount of butter into it, and turned the gas stove on. After cutting about half of the Spam up into thin slices, he placed them into the waiting frying pan.

Because of Kyra's Indian heritage, she'd been raised vegetarian, and Ben had mostly adopted this diet. Although some of her family members allowed themselves a small amount of meat here and there,

Kyra was still strict in her adherence to vegetarianism after reaching adulthood, but not for religious reasons.

Krya was happy to learn that the first time Ben visited the cabin on a so-called hunting expedition was when he'd made the decision to never hunt or kill any animals. All his friends must have come to the same conclusion because they had spent every trip since then drinking and hanging out. No one had bothered to bring a bow or a rifle for the past four years, but they persisted in calling each outing a hunting trip.

Even with all this in his mind, the pull of a nostalgic favorite won out for this meal. It didn't take long for the slices to begin sizzling and the accompanying fragrant smoke to fill the kitchen. It reminded him of being a child.

He soon dug in to two Spam sandwiches, eating them with the voracity of a starving man. The aches and pains of his earlier adventure started melting away, as did the cloudy sensation in his mind. *It's crazy what not eating can do to a person. I really need to stop doing that.*

As was his custom, he cleaned the dishes before leaving the kitchen, and then entered the dining room, flicking on the few available light switches as he went. The sun was almost completely down now, and the cabin always became a vacuum of darkness at night. He went over to the fireplace mantel and poked around through the various items that had been left there over the years.

His searching initially appeared to be fruitless, but Ben was pleased when he dug out a deck of cards.

I can't remember the last time I played solitaire.

He placed the cards out across the small kitchen table and played several unsuccessful games in a row. He took a bathroom break halfway through the game he intended to be his last. Before leaving the table, he glanced one more time at the cards sitting face up. It didn't look good, and he knew he was about to lose his seventh game in a row.

The toilet flushed and the sink sputtered to life, quickly followed by his return through the kitchen into the dining room. Ben sat down at the table morosely, ready to lose yet another game. His eyes fluttered to the cards, followed by an immediate double-take. They were all lined up in perfect rows, every card having been used and the game having been won.

"What the...?"

He looked around and tried to attune all his senses at once to the mystery. It was clear no one else had entered the cabin and he was still alone. So how could this be explained? Had he gotten lost in his thoughts again and failed to realize he was winning for once? That didn't seem likely, especially when he remembered he'd taken a glance at the game in front of him before leaving for the bathroom.

A slight sense of apprehension bloomed in his chest, but it was nothing compared to that which he'd felt earlier in the day. There was nothing sinister or potentially harmful about winning a game of solitaire. Still, he fixated on how much the cards had changed.

How is that possible?

The rational part of him that kept struggling to stay in control did a quick analysis of the situation. *I'm exhausted. Being this tired would make anyone start seeing stuff. Tired eyes can't be trusted.*

CHAPTER SIX

Two Years Ago

"Am I ever going to meet your mom?" Kyra asked.

"Um, yeah... probably not," Ben said evasively.

"What do you mean probably not?" Kyra's tone was light and playful, but she also had an inquiring look.

"Well, you see, I haven't even seen her in years, and I'm not so sure she wants to see me, which could make it difficult for you to meet her, you know?"

"No," Kyra said. "I don't think I do know. What's wrong, Ben?"

Sensing his discomfort, her eyebrows furrowed with worry for a second before she attempted to lighten the mood.

"What's the matter, are you afraid I'll say something to embarrass you?" The lyrical quality of her voice was light with an attempt at humor. Ben usually responded well to this tactic, but this time, her attempt fell flat.

Kyra's eyebrows creased again. Her intuition told her that jokes weren't a good idea, nor was prodding the wisest approach. She moved closer to him on the couch and began running her fingers through his hair.

"I'm here, Ben," she said, her words infused with compassion.

After a couple of false starts and several deep breaths, Ben launched into the story he'd been dreading for months.

"Okay, you know my parents split up and my father wasn't exactly nice to me."

Kyra nodded, squeezed his hand, and kept any initial thoughts to herself.

"Something about my dad never made any sense to me. You see, the early photos of my parents are beautiful. There's so much love between the two of them, and he appears to be so attentive and even sensitive. Sometimes, I think I can remember brief flashes of this behavior toward me. I don't know if it's wishful thinking or if there actually was a time when he didn't constantly seek to punish me for the sin of existing."

Kyra squeezed Ben's hand again. The pain in his voice made her almost regret asking, but she also understood he needed to share all this as much as she needed to hear it. With a nod and a loving look, she coaxed him into continuing his journey through the past.

"I know that he was a total bastard by my seventh birthday. He didn't show up until the last half of my party that year, and when he did make an appearance, he was drunk and mean as hell. Other parents looked at me as if to say, 'this is your fault,' while they gathered their kids and left. Several of those kids never hung out with me again. After that, Dad often came home drunk, and Mom started to cry a lot.

"I remember them arguing most nights. There were a few times when I heard scary noises that I now know accompanied physical abuse. She never told me what really happened, and she always had a good cover story for any wounds that I could see. I think he hid a lot of them, too, by hitting her in areas that were easily covered. He was such an asshole I wouldn't be surprised if the abuse was also sexual."

Kyra cringed. Anger and discomfort wafted from her body, and she kept clenching her free hand into a fist and then releasing it. Ben saw how it was affecting her and tried to stop.

"No," she said. "Please, keep going."

He hesitated, but her angry, cloud-covered eyes cleared long enough to give him an imploring push. With a deep sense of unhappiness, Ben returned to his story.

"This went on for years. I can't tell you how many times I caught my mom crying, only to have her put on a cheerful face as soon as she spotted me. By the time I was fourteen, she'd reached her limit of abuse and ran out the front door during one of their daily fights. I didn't hear anything else about her for months."

Kyra's eyes widened. "Months? Oh Ben, I'm so sorry. What happened?"

"There are several versions of the story, so I don't know for sure if I have the full truth. What I do know is that some local police officers found her wandering down a road several miles away in the middle of the night. According to the report they filed, she was delirious and kept talking to someone or something that wasn't really there. It didn't take long to get her committed, and she's been in a mental health facility ever since."

Tears filled both of their eyes as Kyra wrapped her arms around Ben. "What do the doctors say?"

A look of remorse and hostility transformed his face.

"After turning eighteen, I was able to visit her. One of the nurses filled me in, and it left me praying for some form of retribution against my father. Her official diagnosis is complex trauma, which they believe developed due to the abuse she suffered. Somewhere between the moment she fled the house and when she was found several hours later, she also had some type of psychotic break. It's been almost fifteen years, but she still hallucinates from time to time."

His voice faltered, and he looked to her for comfort. Without saying anything, her left hand returned to stroking his hair and her soft, concerned eyes met his.

"I've gone to visit her at least a dozen times, but she's only agreed to see me once. She seemed perfectly normal at first, but then she started saying things that didn't make any sense to me. She also stopped midsentence at one point, followed by staring off at something that wasn't there. The panic in her eyes was indescribable. By the end, she tried to physically run away from whatever demons are in her head.

After that visit, one of the staff members told me that the mere mention of my name left her agitated for days. They suggested I don't return until there has been some marked improvement in her condition, so I haven't," he shrugged.

"I did get a letter from her once, but it made less sense than some of the stuff she said in person."

"Ben... if I had known, I never would've... thank you for telling me, my love. I can't imagine how hard this has been on you. I'm here if you ever need to talk about it, and I'll be by your side when the time comes to try to visit her again."

A single tear trailed down his cheek as he rested his head on Kyra's shoulder. He didn't say anything for several minutes. When Ben finally broke the silence, he said, "I'm starving. Do you want to order a pizza?"

Knowing the door was shut for now, and possibly forever, Kyra responded, "That sounds good."

CHAPTER SEVEN

Present Day

When Ben reached for his morning cup of coffee, his left hand grazed against the mug.

"Ow! What the..." he asked his hand before noticing the tiny burn where his pain originated. Puzzled, Ben stared at the offending spot, willing it to respond. When that didn't work, he tried pondering the unexpected appearance of the burn, but this tactic brought him no answers.

Must have burned myself while cooking and not noticed it.

Ben shrugged off the mystery of the random burn, along with the blank spots in his memory from the day before. Craving adventure, he took the little aluminum boat out on the water. He didn't fish, but he had always enjoyed passing time in the morning on a boat. After three tries, he got the small motor to come to life, then pushed off from the shore.

Trolling around the lake, Ben enjoyed the early morning fog and the appearance of several different birds, including the majestic bald eagle that almost always started its day by flying in a counter-clockwise motion around the lake. He had only seen it deviate from this course a time or two in the past, so it was with a sense of bewilderment that he witnessed the eagle break its typical routine this morning.

Instead of completing its circular path, it dove feet first into the water and slipped beneath the surface. By the time Ben realized what had happened, the eagle burst back out of the water carrying a fish between its talons. As the bird flew out of sight, a smile came to Ben's lips.

He enjoyed the serenity of the early morning lake as the sun moved across the sky. A rumbling in his stomach broke his reverie, and he maneuvered the boat back to the shore and anchored it once more.

Unwilling to spend any unnecessary time indoors, he poured himself a bowl of cereal and went back to the dock. Only a couple of bites later, Ben fumbled with the Styrofoam bowl.

"SHIT!"

He mournfully watched the meal slip out of his grasp and fall into the water. He'd always cared about keeping the lake clean, but Kyra's love of the environment had further impressed upon him the importance of not getting lazy in a situation like this. Sure, it was only a Styrofoam bowl, but allowing himself to not retrieve it could damage some of the water life. He lamented the loss of the ceramic bowls that had been broken in an accident a year or so ago. Why hadn't they replaced them?

While peeling off his shoes and socks, Ben thought back to the last time he'd stepped into this water. Kyra was with him, and they were laughing about something they'd read in the local paper.

I miss her so much.

He glanced around, knowing that no one would be within eyesight, then pulled his pants off.

No sense in getting my jeans soaked.

He sat back down on the dock, then scooted himself off the edge. As always, the lower temperature of the water was shocking at first but also invigorating. With a determined face, Ben walked around the side of the dock to grab his bowl. The ground squelched underneath his feet, and he soon found it difficult to keep moving forward due to the ever-thickening presence of seaweed.

Yuck.

Ben had loved water since childhood, but the sensation of water plants getting between his toes always grossed him out. When he was a kid, his father convinced him seaweed was a living, breathing creature that would wrap around his feet, pull him under, and cause him to drown. Of course, the cure for this was to move faster, which he later understood meant his dad was attempting to speed up the process of getting deeper into the lake.

Glancing around, he realized the bowl had somehow drifted out of view. Puzzled, he cocked his head to one side while pondering the possibilities.

Ah-ha! Of course! It went UNDER the dock.

Pleased with the solid detective work that had enabled him to solve the mystery of the missing bowl, he knelt and started to reach for it. What his hand grabbed was not Styrofoam, though; it felt slimy and wriggled in his hand. He instinctively let it go before stumbling backward.

Okay, come on. Get a grip. It was just a fish or something.

Approaching the dock once more, Ben decided he would kneel so he could see his target. His knees sunk a bit into the sand, resulting in the disturbing sensation of seaweed brushing against his legs. Still, this method provided instant results as the bowl was now visible about one foot away. Scooching forward on his knees a few more inches, Ben reached for the piece of litter that had once contained his meal.

Damn. It was still out of reach, so he had to duck down and draw closer to the dock's edge.

Success!

The waterlogged Styrofoam threatened to break in his grasp, but he managed to pull it free of its hiding place intact. Ben smiled and turned a bit away from the dock. He walked a few paces through the seaweed, gaining confidence as his desired destination drew nearer.

His right foot stepped forward once more, but this time it didn't find any purchase on the sandy, seaweed covered surface. Instead, his left foot was yanked out from behind him, and he fell face forward into the water. Terror overwhelmed his mind as he became inexplicably certain that the dock monster he'd envisioned during childhood had come to life and captured him.

Ben's body thrashed violently in the water. He grabbed several handfuls of sand and seaweed from the bottom of the lake in a desperate bid to stop his backward trajectory, but his efforts were all fruitless. Slowly but surely, he was pulled back under the dock.

Unable to see his attacker, Ben's hands reached above him and kept hitting the underside of the dock. Before he could make sense of what was happening, the water plants sprang to life and wrapped around his body. Terrified, he became aware that it was getting harder and harder to breathe.

Each time Ben pushed his head above the shallow water, something pulled it back under again. The struggle to get free intensified with each passing second, and the seaweed somehow managed to slither up his legs, around his abdomen, and up his neck.

Another attempt at breaking free of his slimy restraints gave the living seaweed a push in the worst possible direction; it entered his mouth, resisted his screams, and made its way down his throat. His lungs were crippled by the combination of air loss and the invading force that threatened to choke him to death from the inside. Before insentience could take over, he spotted his worst nightmare brought to life. There, in all its glory, was the prideful, twisted visage of the dock creature.

It's real, his mind cried as the last of his air supply ran out.

A sadistic giggling emerged, which had the tonality of a perfect blend between his father and *The Lord of the Ring*'s Golem. Weakened by all his recent struggles, a voice deep in his mind told him to give up. Tempted, he went dormant, and the confused seaweed loosened its grip on his dying body.

This was enough to jump-start Ben's survival instinct; with one last full body thrash, he broke free. Half-crawling and half-running, he stumbled onto the shore and collapsed while coughing up bloody seaweed.

Just as Ben's coughing began to settle down, he noticed the temperature had dropped. Rolling on his back, he caught a glimpse of the clouds. Their shapes had become sinister, and they were turning darker by the second. Sensing the coming storm, he struggled to his feet and headed indoors to take shelter.

The storm rolled in with such haste that he was crossing the backdoor's threshold when the first rain drops fell. They were slow at first but rapidly picked up steam. The interior of the cabin took on the darkness of midnight as thunder ripped through the sky and lightning brought temporary flashes of daylight.

CHAPTER EIGHT

18 Months Ago

Ben and Kyra drove into his small, conservative hometown. The oppression of the single-story buildings and accompanying small minds was inescapable, but it was hard for him to fully appreciate how nerve-wracking this experience might be for Kyra. Despite this, she had stood firmly by his side and insisted on coming with him to his father's funeral.

They arrived in town a few hours early and parked in the downtown area. Ben opted to show Kyra where he'd grown up, even though he had no love for it. As a child, he'd never really questioned the lack of racial diversity because it was all he'd ever known. By the time he'd reached puberty, he realized there was something unsettling about being in a town that was proud to have an almost exclusively white demographic.

The woman at his side, with her dark olive skin tone and warm brown hair, was considered exotic in his hometown, which locals didn't see as a good thing. Although Ben remembered what life had been like here during his teens, he wasn't prepared for people to have an issue with Kyra merely walking down the sidewalk.

Adults of all ages openly gawked as soon as the couple's feet exited his car. Frustrated but determined to push forward, he squeezed her hand and they continued their early afternoon stroll.

Ben put on a show of indifference, or at least he hoped so, but his cheeks also started to get a bit hot under the weight of so many stares. Now he understood why Kyra had been hesitant to do anything other than go straight to the funeral parlor.

Most people kept their unkind thoughts to themselves. He did see a few looks of shock on the faces of those who recognized him as a hometown boy who was so pale that it seemed like he was allergic to the sun. A bigot with a bigger mouth than the capacity for self-control spotted them after a few minutes, and he shattered the stunned silence with ugly cruelty.

"Ben? Is that you, boy? We always knew you were odd, but we didn't know you were a Muslim lover, faggot."

Kyra stiffened at his side, and he started to slow down, intent on replying to the ridiculous commentary. Before he could say anything, she gripped his arm more closely, looking for stability but also non-verbally pleading with him to stay quiet. Sensing her acute discomfort and dealing with plenty of his own, Ben acquiesced to her request.

His internal struggle raged on, though.

Let me guess – everyone who has even slightly dark skin is a Muslim terrorist to you, right? And even though I'm with a woman, I'm still gay? Way to go, Dad. You dragged me back to this land of ignorance one more time. Bastard.

Without talking about it, the two instinctually walked back toward Ben's car. They crossed the street, hoping to avoid another encounter with the boisterously loud, middle-aged, balding white man who looked like he'd had a few too many beers with lunch. The man still eyed them with disgust, but whatever he said this time was mumbled to himself.

Driving to the funeral parlor provided a brief respite, but it also made it clearer than ever that Ben was woefully unprepared to protect his fiancée during these situations. His cheeks burned red again with self-shaming and a sense of inadequacy, but Kyra took his hand and said, "Ben, don't beat yourself up."

"But..." he interjected, only to be cut off.

"Stuff like this happens sometimes. It's not fair, but I've learned that responding makes things much worse. I'm not willing to give jerks like that the pleasure of knowing they've upset me," she finished firmly.

He sat in silence for a moment absorbing her words. Kyra was usually softer-toned and tended to look for the best in everyone. However, when she got heated up or passionate about something, she was a firecracker that couldn't be contained by a single night's sky.

"Okay, I hear what you're saying, and I understand."

She smiled and looked at her fiancé with compassion as he parked the Honda.

"I know this day must be hard enough for you, Ben. We don't need to talk about this any further."

He shook his head, looked her in the eyes and said, "It's not as hard as you might think. Every time I try to find some hidden well of love for my father, it's just not there. He was awful to me, and his so-called love for my mother caused her to literally go out of her mind. No, the only thing hard about this day is being back here. I can't wait to leave. Part of me is wondering why we aren't leaving right now."

With a knowing nod, Kyra said, "Let's just go in and watch the service. We can leave whenever you'd like afterwards."

Although Ben was expected to sit in the front row and make a speech, he and Kyra took a seat in the back. He declined the opportunity to speak and spent minimal time with his father's body. Kyra witnessed his eyes getting wet a few times, but none of those tears fell.

Within two hours, they were on the ninety-minute drive back to Ann Arbor. Relived to be headed home, Kyra allowed her mind to wander to better things.

Ann Arbor is where Ben and I will get married, raise kids, and grow old together.

CHAPTER NINE

Present Day

At first, the sudden presence of the storm creeped him out. Water dripped from his skin – *Wait, how did I fall into the lake again?* – and he had a lingering sense of something being wrong. When he tried to figure out why he felt this way, he was struck by the discombobulating sensation of battling with an elusive word that teased him by fluttering above the tip of his tongue.

Shrugging, he toweled off and put on new clothes. Before long, he settled into the current mood of the day and discovered how intimidating Mother Nature was being. He had once enjoyed the sounds of a good thunderstorm above most others, but they now brought up savage emotional wounds.

As the storm raged on, his burning need for any type of distraction grew. Ben looked at the fireplace mantel again and spotted an old puzzle. It might not be exciting, but constructing the Golden Gate Bridge out of five-hundred colored cardboard pieces was guaranteed to eat up some of the idle time that the storm had presented him with.

He dumped all the pieces on the table, sorting for the edges first. The border soon fell into place, and then he moved on to filling in the interior pieces. Meanwhile, the storm's wrath intensified and the feeble lighting in the cabin flickered several times before going out altogether.

Wanting to stave off the darkness, Ben rummaged through the cupboards until he found a couple of candles. Setting them up on either side of the puzzle, he lit one match, which brought both candles to life.

An hour passed, during which the storm never even hinted at letting up. With a sense of accomplishment, he fit the last ten puzzle pieces into place with ease, then got up to stretch without looking at the finished product.

He took a quick walk around the cabin to get his blood flowing, then returned to the living room. Peering down at the puzzle, he got the vaguest gut feeling that something wasn't quite right. He verified all the pieces had been used and were all in the right spots. Everything was perfect in that regard.

Something's not right. But what? He picked up one of the candles and held it in close for a better look.

There, in the lower left portion of the puzzle. Could it be?

Yes, it appeared the photograph that had been used to design this puzzle had captured one of the many suicides to occur off the venerable bridge. He was stunned. *How could that have made it past the proofing stage?*

The worst part was the haunted look on the woman's face. The more he stared at the puzzle, the more pronounced the image became. His moral center gnawed at him, commanding that he put the puzzle away, but something morbid deep within him would not let him do so. After staring at it for another moment, he forcibly tore himself away.

The storm finally weakened, and he went out into the enclosed porch to watch it leave the lake. He deeply inhaled the freshness of sodden soil. As the sky lightened once again, he noticed the rain had been so heavy that it had caused the water level to rise above its normal point. There was no threat of a flood, but it would probably take a couple days for the level to evaporate down to its normal resting spot.

The massive, crashing waves the wind pushed against the shore caused a large amount of water to splash up into the boat and onto the dock. Frowning, he realized a strong wind would bring about the same result until the excess water receded.

So much for spending his idle time by the lake. It was one thing for the dock to get soaked during a rainstorm, but it was quite another for it to happen when the sky was clear and blue. He hoped the tide would go down faster than he anticipated.

As the afternoon turned into evening and the skies darkened yet again, his stomach come back to life with renewed vigor. The electricity had returned, so he settled on some soup. On his way into the kitchen he paused in front of the puzzle, looking for the suicidal woman who had been floating through his thoughts.

At first, Ben couldn't find her.

Is there such a thing as a storm-induced hallucination?

His eyes eventually fell on something that had most definitely not been there the last time he'd looked at the puzzle. The woman was no longer captured in mid-jump; instead, waves cascaded out from her entry point and only half of her head was still above water.

"What?" It struck him that he'd been saying that an awful lot lately.

In a daze, he walked away from the puzzle, made some soup, and hoped that he had just been having another hunger hallucination. By the time his bowl was empty, Ben's hunger was satiated. He tentatively approached the puzzle once more. His eyes instantly fell upon the place where the woman had been. She wasn't there anymore. Deeply relieved, he lit up a post-meal cigarette.

Ben also decided this was the perfect opportunity to touch base with his best friend, Doug. The two of them had known each other since the fourth grade when Doug's family moved into town. They had both been gawky then; Ben was rail thin and painfully shy. Meanwhile, Doug's young frame was plump and almost always covered by the same hand-me-down jeans and blue short-sleeved button-up shirt.

The two boys grew up in the poor part of town, but that didn't matter to them. They'd become closer with age, and Ben had stood by his friend's side during his wedding day. The plan was for Doug to do the same thing in return for Ben, but fate changed everything.

Of all Ben's friends, Doug had showcased the most patience and empathy with the grieving process. He might have trimmed down his belly, bulked up his body, and become the leader of the football team during their teen years, but Doug never looked down upon his friend's awkwardness. They trusted each other with their deepest, darkest secrets, and this trust had never been broken.

When Ben reached out to Doug, he knew his friend would answer. This was a simple fact of life that had never wavered, so he was a bit surprised when his call went straight to voicemail.

Maybe he's out of range or at the movies or something.

"Hey Doug, it's Ben. I... well, I didn't go to Virginia Beach. I went to Cabin Green. I know, I know... not a good idea, right? I just needed to be near her somehow. I don't know if you can understand, but this is what I need. Anyway... call me back, okay? Bye."

With the phone call made, Ben waited for the inevitable return call from Doug. He prepared to explain how his plans had changed so dramatically. Three days ago, he'd loaded up his car and headed south to spend a couple of weeks at a resort in Virginia Beach.

The place Ben had selected was right on the ocean, included all his meals, and even had free spa services. In truth, it was exactly the type of resort Kyra would've enjoyed, even though she would have felt guilty about it. Meanwhile, he had always been a bit weirded out by the concept of letting strangers pamper him.

His destination was almost twelve hours away by car, but he'd insisted on not only going alone but also driving. He was supposed to break the trip up with a brief furlough at a nice hotel halfway to Virginia Beach. However, all this had changed when he pulled into a rest area a mere hour away from home and called the resort.

His reservation was canceled before *What Sarah Said* by Death Cab for Cutie finished playing on his car stereo. With no further consideration to the potential pros and cons of his new plan, Ben had reversed his driving direction, cruised back past his home, and kept going.

He'd been searching for the comfort that only Kyra could provide, and that directed him toward Cabin Green. He didn't know if

Doug or anyone else could understand, but he did know Doug wouldn't rake him over the coals for it.

Before he knew it, he'd spent so much time reflecting on the past that a full ashtray sat at his feet. It made him a bit uneasy that Doug still hadn't returned his call.

Needing some fresh air, he walked outside and sat down upon the top step. To his surprise, the step wobbled, but this didn't prompt him to move. His head was too preoccupied by being as fuzzy as an old TV stuck on an empty channel. Undeterred by this, the synapses that were still firing correctly set themselves to the task of analyzing the puzzle situation in hopes of finding an answer to what he'd seen.

There had been so many strange things over the past couple of days. He'd somehow managed to see past all of them so far, but he was starting to struggle a bit with feelings of insanity. What if the things he'd seen weren't due to a lack of food or sleep? What if his original instinct on the first night had been accurate? Was there something wrong with the cabin?

CHAPTER TEN

Twelve Years Ago

"Welcome to Banks Psychiatric Care," the robust desk attendant chirped, with much more enthusiasm and warmth than Ben expected. "How can I help you, sir?"

Ben choked back the urge to laugh at being called sir while glancing at her nametag. It reported that her name was Rose, which seemed to be a perfect fit.

"I'm here to see my mother, Sara Tremblay."

"Okay, and what's your name?"

"Ben. Um, Benjamin. Tremblay."

"Is this your first time here, Ben?"

"Uh, yeah. Yes, it is."

He glanced furtively at his feet in a failed attempt to cover up his embarrassment. Visiting his mother in what was basically a psychiatric nursing facility was bad enough, but it was even worse to admit he hadn't been here even once during the past four years.

Her voice took on a quieter, gentler tone as she tried to reassure him that coming at any point was better than never coming at all. "Your mother will understand. She's told me all about you, you know. Didn't you just have your eighteenth birthday?"

Ben nodded in agreement, but the direction of their conversation left him uncomfortable.

"Why, I bet that's the reason you're visiting for the first time now! In fact, I'd bet my left leg on it. I know all about your dad, Ben. It's okay."

She patted his arm and gave him a sympathetic look that reminded him of the school nurse who had tended to his wounds when he was beaten up by bullies in the third grade. The next year, when Doug arrived, most of the physical harassment stopped.

Not trusting himself to speak, Ben swallowed hard and nodded again. Rose seemed placated by this gesture. She picked up the phone, pressed only three buttons, and informed whoever picked up that he was there. Once the call was completed, she escorted him to a small room down the hall.

Rose knocked and turned the knob without waiting for a response. "Well, there you are. I'll give you some privacy. Stay as long as you'd like, dear," she said.

Ben found himself looking into his mother's eyes for the first time in four years. He was overwhelmed with an indescribable emotion that was somewhere between joy, chagrin, and terror. From the look on her face, she was going through something similar.

"Son," her tone sounded flat. A half-second later, emotion flooded her voice. "I've missed you so much."

Without giving it any thought, the two of them met each other in the midpoint of the room and shared an embrace. She put her left hand on the back of his head, pulled him closer, and cried lightly on his shoulder. Although Ben was happy to see his mother, he also had a difficult time dealing with such a big display of her emotions.

"Mom..." he hesitated. "I...I've missed you too. And I'm sorry."

She pulled away just far enough to look into his eyes again. "No. Don't. You have *nothing* to apologize for. This is all his fault."

Ben's gaze returned to the ground. He was infuriated by everything he knew his father had done, but he was also afraid to learn more details.

Please don't tell me anything else. I can't handle it.

Seeing her son's reaction, Sara intuited what had brought such a troubled look to his face. "Don't worry, Ben. I won't waste any more breath on *him*. Tell me what's been going on with you. I've missed so much, and *I'm* sorry."

He spent the next half hour filling her on his high school graduation, eighteenth birthday, and acceptance letter from the University of Michigan. This was all a mere lead-up to what he really wanted to say. Finally, he gathered his courage and asked, "How are you?"

She looked at him quizzically and said, "I'm fine, son. In fact, I'm better than fine. It's so good to spend time with you!"

"Yeah, it's good to spend time with you, too. But that's not what... I mean, how have you been feeling? Since getting here?"

Dark clouds filled her eyes and her jaw tightened.

"Oh," she said, without any of her former enthusiasm and emotion. "You mean am I still crazy, right? Isn't that right?" Her voice didn't get any louder, but the terseness in it made him feel like a young boy getting scolded for breaking the rules.

"Mom, I didn't mean to upset you. I don't really know what happened. I mean, yes, I know that Dad is an asshole who hurt you way too many times. Aunt Vicky told me you had, well, an episode brought on by dealing with his crap for too long. And I can understand that. I have no idea how you put up with it for as long as you did."

"Victoria has no idea what she's talking about and should keep her damn mouth shut," Sara roared.

"Mom..." He cleared his throat. "Here's the thing; I've heard Aunt Vicky's version of events, I've read the police report from that night, and I even got what I'm sure is a bullshit explanation from Dad. What I want is to hear what happened from you. I love you, Mom."

His eyes were misty, and his shoulders slumped with the strain of allowing himself to be so emotionally open with her.

"I'm *not* crazy Ben. I know what you must have been told, but it's a lie."

"But... I mean, why are you *here*?" He looked around in disdain and disbelief.

"Oh, there are worse places I could be. And at least here, he can't hurt me."

"Dad? He'll never hurt you again. I swear it!"

She looked past him, unresponsive.

"Mom?"

"I...," she said before her lips began quivering, followed by a slight tremble that started in her hands but spread like wildfire.

"NO. Go away. You can't be here," she shouted.

"What? Me?"

"Leave me alone." Sara's head cocked to one side.

Is she listening to something?

Her eyes grew huge and her breathing turned ragged. "No. NO. Don't you dare. He's not yours to mess with. Do you understand me? NO! Find someone else to add to your twisted collection."

The door to Sara's room burst open and Rose flew in, accompanied by a burly orderly. Ben had to look away as they forced his mother on top of the bed and injected something into her arm.

"Shh, Sara. You're okay. Nothing's there. Nothing can harm you," Rose said, while stroking the top of Sara's head.

He realized this particular psychotic episode was over when a slight snore emanated from his mother.

"So, that's what they look like, then?"

Rose focused on him for the first time since entering the room. "Yes. She hasn't had one in months, though. We had real hope that they were over for good. Did you say something that upset her?"

"Well..."

"That's that, then," she lamented. "I guess I should have prepared you better or not let you stay so long. It's just that you're the only visitor she's had since being admitted."

The shock on his face made it clear to Rose that Ben hadn't known the rest of his family hadn't visited yet, either.

"Can I ask you something?" he said.

"Sure."

"Is she really crazy? She kept saying she's not and that she could leave at any time."

"It's not my job to decide whether or not she suffers from insanity, Ben. But between you and me, she usually seems more lucid than most. And yes, she could leave at any time. She was only here by mandatory order for the first four weeks."

His eyebrows raised. "Then why...?"

"Why hasn't she left yet? I've asked myself the same question many times," she said.

"Mom claims that staying here keeps her safe from 'him.' Do you know what she means?"

Rose was unable to hide the surprise from her face. "Her ex-husband. Right? I mean, who else could it be?"

CHAPTER ELEVEN

Present Day

The next morning, all the storm clouds from the day before were eradicated from the bluest sky he had ever seen. Ben went about what was becoming a daily routine; he made breakfast, washed the dishes, and took a shower, followed by relaxing on the back porch. Life was moving at a slow pace, and that was exactly what he needed.

The only incident of note was the unusual and sudden appearance of more ivy crawling up both sides of the cabin. This was the first year he'd ever spotted any ivy at all, and it was spreading rapidly. Writing this off as a simple quirk of nature, Ben's comfort levels rebounded.

As the sun began to set amidst a beautiful array of pink and red hues, he returned his attention to the puzzle. It looked completely normal, without any people or unexplainable waves anywhere in the image.

With the sun fully extinguished, an unexpected cold front seeped into the cabin. By eight o'clock, Ben was shivering and had to go out to the wood pile to stock the fireplace. The fire crackled to life as it ate through the newspaper kindling. Heat and light illuminated the living room.

The front of the fireplace had always reminded him of a face, and this was more prevalent when it was fully alight. Shutting down that line of thought before it led somewhere darker, he turned his back to the fireplace and concentrated only on enjoying the warmth. Its fabulousness spread through his limbs, and he reveled in the welcome heat until he fell asleep on the hardwood floor.

The clock signaled the arrival of the witching hour and he awoke with a jolt, accompanied by labored breathing and the rapid beating of his heart. He was suddenly certain an intruder was in the room. His bleary eyes opened wide, and by the scant light of the few lingering embers he investigated every potential hiding spot inside of the cabin.

He came across no one but did find some strange things; most notably, that the puzzle had been moved. It was still complete, but it now sat on the opposite end of the kitchen table. His mouth slackened as he tried to understand what was happening.

With an almost overwhelming sense of trepidation, he moved over to the puzzle and forced himself to look down at it. There, in the lower left corner, was an arm reaching up through the top of the water. He rubbed his eyes, hoping that would take the image away, but it remained steadfast.

"No," he said, followed by an oppressive heaviness and snapping sensation deep inside of his chest. "NO!"

He ripped the puzzle apart, causing the pieces to slide across the table, with many of them clattering to the floor. Acting merely on instinct, he threw himself across the room at the front door and clawed at the doorknob. It wouldn't budge. Frantically, he tried turning it back and forth while simultaneously attempting to pull and shove it open. Nothing worked. Growing hysteria clasped him in an ice-cold vice. Guttural sobs of terror rose in the back of his throat as he continued to pry at the door.

"What the fuck is going on?"

Giving up, he fled toward the back door. He had apparently shut and locked it before he fell asleep, although he had no recollection of having done so. He typically left it open so the breeze from the enclosed porch would filter through the cabin. A split second before falling off the razor thin edge of sanity, Ben remembered how cold it had been and concluded he probably had shut it, regardless of the gap in his memory.

He reached the second door and discovered it also held fast. An overwhelming sense of despair implored him to give up. He responded by sliding to the floor while banging his fists against the uncooperative door. His knuckles scraped open, and his blood mixed with the layer of dust coating his would-be escape route. It was at this exact moment the last embers of the fire burned out, plunging the cabin into pitch darkness. Ben froze, afraid to move or even breathe. The silence was deafening and all pervasive.

He held his breath for as long as humanly possible, concerned that something as minimal as the life-affirming sound of inhalation would give him away. A whining noise developed in his ears and black spots soon entered his field of vision, forcing him to resume a normal breathing pattern.

As he tried to avoid making any other sounds, he noticed an odd scratching noise. It was so faint at first that he tried to convince himself it was just his imagination, but the rapidly escalating volume could not be denied. Fear gripped him like a cold bucket of water, and he was transported back in time to the five-year-old still residing inside him who had been terrified of the dark. Was the boogeyman coming for him?

Ben pulled himself into a shaky ball as the scratching noise somehow intensified even more. He envisioned giant rats that would rip him apart, limb from limb, while dining upon his flesh. A fresh batch of anxiety gripped his mind, and the pace of his beating heart threatened an imminent implosion.

The scratching moved closer with each passing moment. Just as he was certain its maker was less than a foot away, the fireplace roared to life with a fire two times bigger than the one he'd first started. Flames shot out of the metal grate's eyes before receding back into their home. He was paralyzed with fear, and the overly aggressive fire singed his hair. Ben's eyes fell upon the kitchen table. The puzzle was back, and it appeared to be completely formed again.

He turned his head away with vigor before succumbing to an overwhelming compulsion to see what the five-hundred jigsaw pieces were up to now. Against his own will, he rose into a standing position and put one foot in front of the other. His pace was agonizingly slow, with movements stilted in the manor of a marionette. When Ben finally made it to the table, he sat down in one of the old wooden chairs with such force that part of it splintered.

His arms stretched out wide across the table, and his palms pushed down upon it. He did not want to look, but the angle of his neck was forcibly altered by a violently strong push. His nose almost grazed the pieces on the lower left corner as he came face-to-face with the puzzle yet again. It took a second for his eyes to readjust to the closeness of the image. When they did, he saw the waves were now broken by the presence of a large fin. The water itself was clouded with something red, presumably blood.

In shock and disgust, he tried to get up from the table but found himself pinned into position by invisible hands. His eyes wouldn't close under his direction. He was forced to continue staring at the puzzle. What had just been a still image now magically moved. Ripping flesh and the sickening crunch of breaking bones accompanied a shrill scream. A massive great white shark had pounced upon the woman and was greedily enjoying its live bait.

How the hell did she survive the fall? And the first shark bite?

Audible evidence of the woman's pain continued unabated, despite the water's rapid influx of blood. Ben's limbs shook, and he stubbornly tried to pull away again. Failing in his latest attempt, he settled on a new tactic.

Maybe if I lean a bit closer, I can save her.

This idea seemed crazy, but so did the entire situation. Nothing hindered his movements as he lowered his head closer to the puzzle. With a shocking rush of coldness, the tip of his nose entered the frigid water. Petrified, he roughly pulled his head back as far as it would go and saw drops of blood red water fall onto the puzzle. He shrieked and unceremoniously fainted as he finally pulled loose of whatever had been binding him.

CHAPTER TWELVE

Sunlight broke through the few windows in the cabin and highlighted his comatose form. Ben did not jolt awake as one might have expected. Instead, he slowly regained consciousness; stretching first, then flipping from side to side until he opened his eyes.

He was surprised to find himself lying on the floor. The fire was no longer burning and the back door was slightly ajar.

He sat up drowsily and combated wooziness that left him off-kilter. He ran his fingers through his greasy hair. What he wanted more than anything was a strong cup of coffee and a hot shower. While the coffee was brewing, he dared to glance toward the kitchen table.

The puzzle pieces were everywhere, just as they had been the afternoon before when he'd dismantled the disturbing image of the Golden Gate Bridge. This struck him as odd, as did the open back door, for he had the strong suspicion things had not been like that when he'd fallen asleep. He couldn't quite remember for sure though, and decided to shake it off and go about his day.

After drinking not just one cup of coffee but two, Ben took a shower. His freshly washed hair was still dripping wet as he walked over to the kitchen table and purposefully picked up the puzzle box. With a quick swoop of his arm, he knocked the pieces into the box and hastily placed it back on the mantel.

A lethargic air clung to his body, almost like he was hung over but couldn't figure out why. He supposed it had something to do with spending the night on a hardwood floor. Why that had happened was just out of the reach of his increasingly unreliable memory, but he reasoned he'd simply fallen asleep unexpectedly.

His muscles were tense, almost as if in preparation to run away without warning, and he had an overall sensation of lousiness. He thought it would be best to skip his morning boat ride and take a nap on top of an actual mattress.

Ben relaxed upon what now felt like the softest mattress in existence and closed his eyes. Two breaths later, he began drifting into somnolence.

Right before he could pass fully into the land of sleep, he was jarred awake by a falling sensation. This reminded him of a terrifying childhood incident involving a suddenly broken bed spring and an overactive imagination. To his youthful mind, no spring had popped; it was the Devil jumping on his bed, intent on claiming his soul. All these years later, the fear of that moment was reignited whenever his sleep was interrupted.

He took a deep breath to slow down the accelerated pace of his heart. His heavy eyelids closed again and, surprisingly, he immediately drifted back to sleep.

Forty minutes passed uneventfully before his eyelids started to flutter. In his dream, he saw thousands of ghastly looking women jump off a tall bridge and split in half when they hit the water below. He screamed himself hoarse trying to make them come to their senses or to get someone else's attention, but the scene unfolding in front of him would not stop.

From Ben's vantage point, perched on top of a cliff opposite the bridge, there was little else he could do other than scream. The hazy quality of dreams allowed years to pass as he fell to his knees. A wave of complete and utter despair washed over him, and it extracted every drop of liquid from his body until the tears were gone and his body was smooth as stone.

An idea flashed in his mind. He stood effortlessly and walked toward the edge of the cliff. Without the slightest flicker of hesitation, he walked right off the edge. His body stayed still, with his arms at his sides, and he made the plunge toward the waiting water without making a single noise. As the first hint of coldness hit his toes he awoke, sat straight up in bed, and cried out.

He was shocked that he was actually in bed at the cabin instead of in the cold water. A shudder went through his entire body. Ben had been so certain he was about to die that it left him numb and unable to focus on any other thoughts.

The meaning behind the dream eluded him, and it left him nauseated at the suicidal implications. Throughout everything he'd experienced, he had never given into such thoughts – no matter how many times they occurred – and he was proud of this fact. Kyra would not have wanted that for him, and he knew if there was an afterlife, she would be super pissed off at him if he took his own life.

Although he was afraid to dream again, his body gave into exhaustion. Several hours later, his eyes opened in the dark.

Wow, it must be about five-thirty in the morning.

He could no longer remember having woken up earlier that day on the living room floor. This memory, like so many other recent ones, eluded his conscious self.

He turned on the coffee maker and became instantly confused at its insistence that the time was seven o'clock. The darkness outside didn't mesh with his theory that it was early in the morning.

Huh. Maybe a storm is coming.

He stuck his head out the front door and was shocked upon seeing the placement of the sun in the sky. Realizing the time was seven pm., he opted for food instead of coffee

With sustenance warming his stomach, he indulged in a cigarette. Flashes of the nightmare began to return to him as he inhaled the toxic but beloved fumes. It had really been a frightening dream, and he hoped it wasn't a harbinger of things to come. What haunted him the most were the expressions on the faces of the hundreds of identical women who had plunged to their deaths.

The bridge itself was shrouded in mystery. An almost unnaturally thick layer of fog had obscured its identity. He thought he might have seen a brief flash of red, but he wasn't sure enough of it to hazard a guess as to the setting of the dream. He also knew dream locations weren't necessarily based on real places, so he told himself the bridge wasn't the important piece of the dream. It nagged him, though, and he couldn't shake the notion that it might represent something important. If only he could figure out what.

Trying to divert the course of his thinking, he grabbed the deck of cards off the mantel and played two games of solitaire; losing the first one but winning the second. The victory put the hint of a sparkle in his eye. His unexpected good fortune uplifted him enough that he didn't spare another thought to the distressing dream while climbing into bed. By the time he reawakened almost twelve hours later, all memories of the dream had been forgotten, along with the oddity of losing a day.

His phone indicated he had no new messages, but that didn't seem unusual. It was hard to get a signal in the cabin, and his friends thought he was enjoying a fancy resort. Like many of his other recent memory gaps, calling Doug had been erased from his mind.

On the bright side, Ben's strength and mental clarity had rebounded, and nothing sounded better than getting back on the water. Therefore, he wasted little time before practically leaping down the path to the boat.

The motor came to life with one yank of the cord and he hopped in, looking forward to another chance to watch the wildlife and soak in some sun. It was the warmest day of his trip by far, and he wanted to revel in it. He'd slept far too late to see the bald eagle, but the resident loons were out and about, offering up their eerie song for his buoyantly attuned ears.

Once the loons had departed the immediate area, Ben reached down into the boat, picked up a couple of round stones, and began skipping them on the water. He chuckled as a fish jumped out of the water in pursuit.

Shortly after the hungry fish swam off to find a more viable meal, the motor cranked back to life and he returned to spinning circles around the little island. Ben looked for any signs of life but saw nothing more than a couple of tiny birds. He cut the motor to allow the natural current of the lake to carry him back toward the shore at a snail's pace.

At approximately one-hundred feet out, something below the surface caught his eye. He peered over the edge of the boat to look for answers, but all he could see was something white and glinting. Typically, he would have passed it by, but something about this particular glint captured his attention.

Ben put the anchor into the water and reached overboard. His hand brushed against something hard and presumably unnatural. Whatever it was had gotten jammed, and no matter how hard he tugged, it wouldn't come free.

A streak of stubbornness took over, leaving him adamant that it was important to find out what was in the water. He removed his clothing and jumped in.

The frigid water shocked him at first, but he somehow quickly got used to the temperature. Once he became more comfortable, he dove underneath the surface and swam downward.

Upon reaching his goal, Ben was stunned to find a large pile of human bones. His former curiosity was sated instantly as dread overcame his frame. With a struggle, he regained just enough control of his limbs to swim back to the surface. Panicked, he grabbed the side of the boat and clambered back inside of it.

"Holy fuck!"

In less than sixty seconds, he had the anchor back in the boat, the engine roared to life, and he took off at maximum speed capacity.

As soon as he reached the shore, he jumped out of the boat and ran into the cabin, slamming the door behind him. Several different scenarios ran through his mind at a breakneck pace, and he had difficulty honing in on one idea. It was clear something horrible had happened here, but this didn't necessarily mean foul play had been involved.

He tried to calm down and found that he was shivering. The only thing he could think of that would warm him up was a hot shower. Before turning the shower water on, he debated with himself; *maybe I should skip the shower and go straight to the police.* However, the need for warmth overcame him, and he got into the hottest shower he'd taken since arriving at the cabin.

The water rained down upon Ben's skin, but despite his hopes, it didn't have even the slightest internal warming effect. His mind obsessively picked at the mystery of what he had found and how it had ended up in the lake.

Why would a pile of human bones, presumably enough to belong to multiple people, reside inside the lake? Had there been some kind of boating accident? Had the local cemetery been full or suffered some type of run off incident? Had it perhaps been the chosen final resting place of the family that used to own the cabin?

Lost in thought, he stood in the shower for almost an hour and used up every drop of hot water. It made no difference because he was still as chilled when he stepped out of the shower as he'd been when he had entered it.

Indecision plagued him. He could try to do his best to forget what he'd seen, or he could go into town and report his discovery to the police. Something in the back of his mind adamantly didn't want him to choose the latter option. It was an unidentifiable form of paranoia he'd never encountered before.

Pondering it for a few moments, he was surprised to unravel the truth; he was petrified he would somehow be viewed as a suspect. It was preposterous because who in their right mind would lead the police to the scene of their own crime? Still, he couldn't shake free of the paranoia.

While deliberating, Ben paced the floor and cigarette smoke swirled around his head. He soon concluded it was too risky to involve the police. He also knew he couldn't take the risk of anyone else discovering the bones that close to his cabin. The only viable solution he could think of was to remove the unidentified bones from the water and bury them elsewhere.

"Yes," he said. "That's exactly what I should do."

Seizing on to this idea like it was the next great American novel, he selected the island as a suitable location. Although his area of the lake was private, the occasional fisherman would troll by, so it wouldn't be wise to begin the excavation during the day.

A muffled voice echoed in his head, seemingly from a long distance.

Wait, what? Why am I going to move the bones instead of going to the police? This is a terrible plan.

He started grappling with this question, but an expeditious fog settled over his mind, breaking Ben free of his uncertainty.

"Doing this is the only thing that makes sense."

With the decision-making process out of the way, Ben had no other choice than to go about the rest of his day. After enjoying a light lunch, he headed outside. In years past, a daily stroll through the woods had been among his favorite cabin area activities, and he was surprised when he realized he hadn't taken one yet.

The trail he selected was a one-mile hike. That seemed like a good way to pass the time and burn off some off his nervous energy. He passed several wildflower patches and spotted numerous species of birds and small animals.

At about the halfway point, Ben encountered an unusually talkative chipmunk who disparaged him for walking through its home. With an amused expression, he sat down upon an old, fallen log, therefore giving the chipmunk something to really yell at him about. The chattering sound caught the attention of a half-dozen squirrels that ran past his feet.

He blissfully took it all in and found himself mulishly protective of the land and all its inhabitants. The choice he had made was now solidified. It wasn't much of a leap to imagine how damaging a police investigation would be to the land. They would tramp through the woods, scare off the animals, and leave far too many traces of themselves behind when they finally left.

He sat relatively still for long enough that the chipmunk grew bored and ran off, leaving him to enjoy the silence. Ben continued to sit there until the sun had crossed almost all the way across the sky.

His plan was a simple one; he was going to take the boat out, sans motor, to the place where the bones were hidden. He would dive into the water and remove them. Once the boat was filled, he would row it over to the island where he would bury the evidence.

Ben returned to the cabin and shined a flashlight into the crawl space. He tried not to think about the many spiderwebs while he reached his arm deep enough to grab a hidden shovel. A moment later, he placed the shovel inside the boat and pushed off from the shore while jumping in.

The current was as still as a stagnant pond, and the starless sky plunged his surroundings into almost complete darkness. Experience told him the inky blackness of the sky was absolute enough that it would prevent anyone more than ten feet away from seeing him as long as he kept the flashlight turned off.

Slowly, with a conscious effort to not make much noise, he paddled the boat over to what he'd become confident was the scene of a crime. He dropped the anchor in the water once again and readied himself to dive into the cold, murky lake.

He hesitated long enough to count to three before taking in a lungful of air and thrusting himself downward. When he hit the lake bed, he opened his eyes and looked around. The blackness of the night penetrated the lake, making it impossible to see anything, including the bones. He reached around to orient himself but found nothing.

Without wasting any more time, he surfaced and reached inside the boat. He mentally congratulated himself for having a waterproof flashlight, which he'd fortuitously purchased several years ago for a nighttime swimming expedition.

Holding tightly to the flashlight, Ben swam to the bottom of the lake yet again before turning the light on. It bounced eerily around the water and made the seaweed and rocks look monstrous and huge. As far as the eye could see, though, that was all that was down there.

Stymied, he swam back to the surface, taking care to turn off the light before surfacing again. While treading water, he peered across the lake for the landmarks that would tell him his exact position. What he saw confirmed what he'd already been confident of; he was in the exact same place he'd been earlier today. So where were the bones?

Despite being confident of his placement, he still checked a wide perimeter by diving back and forth between the surface and lake bed. Two hours later, he had found nothing and was chilled nearly to the point of hypothermia. Ben told himself he'd return in the daytime to find the bones.

He carefully tied the boat to the dock before heading inside the cabin. Sleep sounded like the perfect way to restore the massive amount of energy he'd burned off diving and swimming.

He opened the bedroom door, flicked on the light, and walked inside as he pulled the door shut behind him. He turned toward the bed and let out a bloodcurdling scream that could easily be heard half a mile away, if only anyone had been there to hear it.

"What the fuck?"

There, on the bed, was an overflowing pile of wet, human bones. They were obviously old and brittle; the stack that had fallen off the bed had split apart into several smaller pieces.

He almost tore the bedroom door off its frame as he rushed away from the bones. As soon as he crossed over the threshold back into the living room, he slammed the door shut, slid to the ground, and pressed his back against the door in an effort to banish what he'd seen.

How could the bones have been moved from the lake to the bedroom? How could anyone have entered the cabin without me noticing? When was the last time I was even in the bedroom? Before the woods?

It was theoretically possible that someone could have had enough time to put the bones on the bed. The more important questions were why had someone done it and who had that someone been?

As the shock abated, paranoia stole over his entire frame once more. He might not know who or why, but it didn't take much of a leap to decide no one would have done such a thing without a malicious intention.

Perhaps it was the person who'd hidden the bones inside the lake in the first place. Does a killer live nearby? Maybe I was spotted earlier when I first jumped into the water.

The more Ben dwelled on it, the more strongly he believed that the bones' appearance signaled his own impending doom. Whomever had placed the bones there obviously had access both to the lake and to his cabin. That meant it wouldn't be too hard for them to reach him, as well. It also meant if he was being framed, the police could already be on their way.

Could it have even been me? No... right?

With his mind racing, he decided the only practical thing to do was to load the bones into the boat and take them over to the island as he'd originally planned.

* * * * *

It took more than two hours of schlepping back and forth, but he'd finally placed the last of the bones inside the boat. Anxious to get rid of the evidence, he'd left barely enough room for himself to sit.

Still cognizant of attracting unwanted attention, he rowed the boat all the way out to the island and anchored it on the far side so it couldn't be seen from the properties on the shore. Ben's overworked muscles threatened to quit several times, but he pulled all the bones out and carried them to the center of the island without the benefit of any man-made light.

Two-and-a-half hours later, he'd gotten the entire pile of human remains relocated to the most inconspicuous place he could find. Once there, it took another two hours to dig a deep and wide enough hole. The sun poked its head out of the dark horizon by the time he'd covered the bone-filled hole with freshly-turned soil. All the effort he'd expended throughout the night left him exhausted, but he still couldn't rest yet.

Ben cautiously rowed back across the water as the bald eagle flew overhead. As soon as he entered the cabin, his physical and mental exhaustion temporarily overcame his justifiable concerns for his own life and he passed out on the couch.

CHAPTER THIRTEEN

22 Months Ago

Ben introduced Kyra to Cabin Green a month after they started dating, during an unseasonably warm November weekend. These surreptitious trips were among the few times the two of them were able to fall asleep side-by-side. At the time, he had thought it was odd that someone who was so independent and unyielding in her passionate beliefs was also willing to conform to an old-fashioned view of propriety regarding relationships.

Later, he figured out she maintained her adamant stance against moving in together before marriage because this was the only way she could remain true to her parents' wishes. It became clear she didn't share this viewpoint, but it was also obvious she made this concession to honor cultural traditions.

Fortunately, a few nights away in the cabin every so often didn't count as living together. The first time Kyra saw Cabin Green a delighted look almost overwhelmed her face.

"It's fantastic, Ben! This is so much better than I imagined. The solitude, the lake, the woods," she trailed off while continuing to investigate the property. "Wow, is that an island I see in the lake?

"Yes," Ben said. "Do you want me to take you there later?"

Her eyes sparkled mischievously. "Is it as isolated as it looks?"

"Definitely. None of the other nearby cabin owners appear to be here this weekend, so there's no one else who has access to the island."

"Then I hope you've got a bottle of wine, some type of picnic basket, and a comfortable blanket in the cabin because we're going to need to eat lunch there. Followed by having some fun, of course."

The strong flirtatious energy coming off her in waves would have been enough to make Ben drive hours away to pick up the supplies she'd listed. The good news was he didn't have to go to extremes because the cabin was equipped with everything on Kyra's wish list.

This is going to be a great weekend.

Grinning, he reached for her hands and pulled her near as he pressed his lips against the softness of her forehead.

"I'm so glad you're here."

* * * * *

The next day, they loaded up a picnic lunch, along with a thick blanket, and took off on the boat. The crispness of the air surprised him.

I guess we'll just have to warm each other up.

Kyra was clearly on the same page, and the two of them started kissing before they managed to sample their food or the wine.

After making love, she serenely laid her head on his chest.

"I love you, Kyra."

"I know."

Less than a beat later, she laughed at her pop culture joke. He joined in, and their laughter continued unabated for so long they both ended up clutching their stomachs and gasping for air.

The joke itself wasn't all that funny, even though it did refer to one of their favorite movies, *The Empire Strikes Back*. The root of their mirth was a case of infectious laughter, coupled with the afterglow of having sex.

When they settled down long enough to get their breathing back under control, she looked him in the eyes and said, "I love you."

Unable to control himself, Ben pulled out his best Han Solo impression and replied, "I know." This caused a second round of laughter, but it didn't last quite as long as the first.

"Thank you for bringing me here, Ben. I can understand why this place is so special to you, and it means a lot that you wanted to share it with me."

Without thinking, he said, "Of course. I want to share everything with you."

As the words left his lips, she saw his cheeks redden characteristically as they did whenever he believed he'd spoken out of turn or done something wrong.

They'd only been together for a month, but he'd decided weeks ago she was it for him. No one else could hold a candle to her, and he was already planning his eventual proposal. He didn't want to freak her out by saying too much too soon.

The smile on her face told him he didn't need to worry. Despite his concerns of less than a minute ago, he considered giving into the impulse to propose right then and there. No one could ever say it wasn't a romantic setting, but he became dissuaded when the reality of not having a ring hit him.

No, I'm going to do this right. She deserves that.

* * * * *

The rest of the trip went way too fast, but they squeezed every drop of enjoyment out of their time away together. They had such an easy back and forth with each other; she cooked, and Ben did the dishes. He chopped firewood, and she built a fire far more impressive than any he'd ever put together. Their conversations also flowed as freely as wine at a vineyard tasting.

During the drive home, Kyra asked him if he'd ever considered living in the cabin full-time.

"Sometimes it does seem like the ideal option, but I wonder about living in such a remote place. I mean, yeah, no one bothered us, and that was awesome. But what about when we need to go into town? Are the locals as small-minded as the ones in my hometown? Because if so, I'd have to become a hermit to be happy here."

"I hear you. If it could work, though... just imagine. Waking up every single day to that view. Taking nature walks on the trial. Breathing in the fresher air. There's no factories or plants nearby, nor are there a lot of cars on the road. The air quality is so good that my lungs didn't quite know how to handle it," she laughed.

He contemplated her words, wondering if she was thinking of marriage, too. *Could we really move to Cabin Green after getting married? Would the others let me buy out their share?*

"You know what? You might be right. The positives do outweigh the negatives." Testing the water, he said, "We could grow old and gray there."

She detected a jovial tone in his voice but suspected that was for her benefit in case his words freaked her out. "That sounds lovely, Ben."

His heart skipped a beat, and he became determined to ask her to marry him by their first anniversary so they could begin planning their future together at Cabin Green.

CHAPTER FOURTEEN

Present Day

The air in the cabin was thick and oppressive like a heavy London fog. In a semi-dazed state, Ben stiffly rose from the couch and walked to the dark kitchen. He glanced at the clock – *Wow, I must have slept for almost twenty hours* - before stepping into the bathroom.

With the door closed behind him, he understood for the first time just how uncomfortably small the room was. Others had complained about it in the past, but he'd never really given it much thought before now.

He stared at himself in the dingy mirror while washing his hands. The vision that returned his gaze was startling as the black circles under his eyes had become more pronounced than ever. It seemed improbable that the large amount of sleep he'd gotten hadn't provided some sort of restorative benefits. But somehow, all the evidence showed that getting more rest than he'd had in months had become a hindrance upon his appearance.

Overwhelmed by the desire to see himself in a different light, he splashed cold water on his face. The sensation was pleasing, but once he dried off, Ben saw it didn't make any difference at all. Perhaps more distressing than the black circles was the emptiness that peered back at him from his eyes. They were a lighter shade of green than usual, like almost all the fire had gone out of them.

Ben reflected upon his actions of the previous day. *Did I do the right thing? Was it crazy to have buried those bones?*

Uncertainty plagued him, but he was feeling better about his own safety. After all, he'd slept for an inordinately long time and nothing bad had befallen him. If someone was out to get him, wouldn't they have used that time to cause him harm?

Not if I was the one who...

This thought was interrupted by doubt wafting over him like incense. *I bet it was all just a dream, and I've gotten worked up about nothing.*

The idea of it having been a nightmare was appealing, but it also made him question if he could trust his own memories. This train of thought persistently nagged at him. Before Ben could even completely understand what he was doing, he was on his way to the island to see if he'd really buried something there.

In his haste to see if he'd imagined the crazy events of the past couple of days, he forgot to maintain a level of silence. The engine announced his presence to anyone nearby as he pushed the boat to provide speedy passage. Ben arrived at the far side of the island almost instantly.

He barely took the time to cut the engine and drop the anchor before catapulting himself off the boat and running deep into the island. By the faint light of a cloudy moon, he saw a large mound of dirt. He didn't know what he'd hoped or expected to see, but the mound did prove he'd been here. Now it was time to dig into it and double-check what he'd buried.

His back ached from the trials of the past several days, but Ben's confusion enabled him to make quick work of the loose dirt. He dug down past the spot where he was certain the bones had begun, but there was nothing there. Flustered, he pushed himself to dig even faster.

He made good time, getting near the bottom of the pit in less than forty-five minutes. Still, he found no bones. Rather than being relieved, he began questioning his own sanity. He had been to the island, dug a hole, and then re-filled it. If he hadn't been burying something, what the hell had he done it for?

He tossed the shovel off to his side and sagged down to his knees in the crumbling earth. Tears fell slowly at first but increased until he could no longer see properly. Without any warning, the gut-wrenching pain of guilt and loss washed over him as he sobbed harder while crying out for Kyra. Her remains resided in the ground, and it struck him that perhaps his should, too.

As soon as this thought swooped across his mind, he slid head first into the hole. Forgetting all his previous beliefs about suicide, Ben landed inside the makeshift grave with a thud. He crawled around in the dirt, frantically clawing at it while trying to make it all fall in upon himself.

Most of the dirt he needed was outside of the hole, so he was only able to bury himself up to his knees. Vexed and enraged, he howled as the sun awoke to lighten the sky. His fists beat against the sides of his would-be grave in anger until long after his skin had ruptured and freshly-spilled blood congealed with the dirt. Exhaustion saved him from being able to do any irreparable damage; unconsciousness grabbed Ben as he hovered in a semi-standing, semi-buried state.

The sun lingered high in the sky when he groggily came to in unfamiliar territory. It took a couple moments for his blurry eyes to focus, and once they did, Ben couldn't figure out what he was seeing.

Why am I in a hole? And why am I covered in dirt?

He tried to pull his legs out of the semi-compacted earth, but doing so caused the ground beneath him to shift. Something hard collided with his shins. Startled, he bent down at the waist and put his hands to the task of digging his legs out. What he found was unexpected, although perhaps it shouldn't have been; a human bone rested accusingly against his shins. Letting out a stifled shriek, he yanked his legs the rest of the way out with one quick, terror-filled leap.

Ben's legs were now free of the dirt, but he was still stuck several feet down in a makeshift grave. His eyes searched the hole for any type of a handhold, but none were evident. Ben moved to the farthest side of the grave and stopped looking toward the source of his panic. As a result, he failed to realize it was no longer just a single bone. Instead, a perfectly-formed human skeleton stood right next to him.

Delayed warning bells went off in Ben's mind; someone was looking at him. He turned his head to the far right, and the skeleton came into full view. He screamed like an arachnophobe in a room full of spiders and clawed at the earth around and above him.

Sweat drenched his shirt. Once the realization sunk in that he wasn't getting anywhere, his body froze, and a second scream became muted before it could pass through his lips.

The skeleton didn't move toward him at first, but it did stare at him with its empty eye sockets. The stare was sharper than a knife and oozed hatred and anger. As preposterous as it was, Ben was instantly convinced the skeleton had reanimated with the sole purpose of killing him.

Maybe it had already been buried here and he'd disturbed its sleep, or maybe it had been among the bones that he thought he'd brought here. Either way, it stood upright less than three feet from him, and he had no way of fleeing. Hopelessness rained down on Ben, and he did the only thing that he could think of; he spoke.

"Um... hi."

The skeleton twisted its head to the right and looked at him with an air of curiosity. He wouldn't have thought it possible, but the skull showed a whole world of different emotions.

"Look... I'm really sorry if I disturbed you. I just want to get out of here and leave you alone. Okay?"

The skeleton considered this request before the harshest, most grating sound he'd ever encountered echoed forth from its mouth. It took a beat to realize that the noises were actually words.

"No, that's not okay," it said in an angry voice that was horrifying and unmistakably female. "You killed me, and now it's your turn to die."

"What?" he cried, lunging himself upward but finding nothing to grab onto.

"You know what you did," the voice said. The more it spoke, the more it regained some humanity. "God can't judge you because he's not there, so I'll have to be the one to do it."

The last three words sounded distinctly human. Worse, they sounded familiar. With daggers piercing his heart, Ben said, "W-what? Kyra? Why? How?"

"Yes," she said while moving closer to Ben. Her skeletal arms reached for him and quickly found his neck.

"Please," he implored her. "I didn't mean to disturb you."

"And I won't mean to do this!"

She squeezed. The coldness of her boney fingers tore through his flesh and left him shivering as she crushed his larynx. Soon he could no longer utter any noises, and all the breath had been ripped from his frame. Kyra tossed him to the ground like a rag doll.

A trickle of blood leaked from his nose, but she didn't pay any attention to it. Evidently satisfied, she stepped into the part of the hole with the weakest dirt, sunk downward at a staggeringly fast pace, and disappeared. The earth filled itself back in, covering up any traces of her having been there.

* * * * *

Ben found himself lying on the side of the hole. His head hurt, but other than that, there was no sign of any of the stuff that had just happened. After briefly considering what his memory claimed to be real, he realized Kyra hadn't been there at all. He must have imagined or dreamed the distressing and confusing encounter.

He was unsure how he'd come to be outside of the hole, for he'd been positive he had fallen into it. It was hard to determine what was real, though.

It's probably better to stop trying to figure it out.

With a last glance into the would-be grave, Ben determined it was definitely empty. There were no visible foot prints or indentions in the dirt. Rather than dwell on it any longer, he set to work refilling the hole. It was a long and tiring task, made even more arduous by his lack of adrenaline. Without the fear of something lurking, he had no real reason to work with any level of speed.

According to the sun, less than an hour had passed. His muscles told a different story as he finished his work and stumbled wearily across the island to his boat. Everything seemed normal, which made Ben even more persuaded that the events of the past couple of days had been precipitated by bad dreams.

Perhaps I should spend more time awake.

His dreams had been extra vivid with a splash of craziness for at least a week now, and that couldn't be good for anyone. Since not sleeping wasn't an option, he wondered if there was a way to suppress his dreams for a little while. Ben remembered that back in college he'd taken sleeping pills, and he hadn't had any dreams at all. Maybe that was the answer.

He arrived back at the cabin before concluding he would need to go into town, at least long enough to pick up some sleeping pills. Once the decision was made, it occurred to him he should probably do some laundry and pick up some more food, too. Although he hadn't consciously realized it yet, he was definitely going to stay for longer than a week. He might even stick around for the full two weeks that his friends expected him to be at the Virginia Beach resort.

Before he could think about second guessing himself, he'd gathered up all his clothes and tossed them into the back seat of the car. He soon parked in front of the laundromat. It was just as deserted as it had been the last time, and he was equally relieved by this fact.

While his clothes went through the wash cycle, he had a cigarette at the same table as his last visit. There was no elderly man there to keep him company this time, so he idly checked his iPhone. There were still no calls or texts from Doug. Facebook was oddly quiet, too. Ben sent a quick text to Doug, followed by short messages to his other closest friends and cabin co-owners, Stephen and Mark.

He passed twenty minutes sitting there playing on his phone, during which time he didn't see any cars or people. He surprised himself by feeling a sense of a relief when he saw the cashier inside the Dash-n-Save.

There were three different bottles of sleeping pills on the shelf. He compared their ingredients and settled on a bottle of Tylenol PM. After selecting what would hopefully stifle his dreams, Ben set about the task of restocking the kitchen.

The drive back was uneventful, and he had everything in place within the cabin before the sun went down. It did strike him as odd that the ivy had crawled over more than half the cabin. He was also surprised by darkened, weathered sections of wood he could have sworn weren't there a week ago. His weariness from all the digging and rowing knocked these concerns out of his head, though.

With the freshly laundered sheets on the full-sized bed, Ben decided to test his theory about dreamless sleep. He swallowed two of the cylindrical blue pills and waited for them to work their magic.

CHAPTER FIFTEEN

Ben was surprisingly refreshed and a lot less sore than he'd anticipated. There had been no disturbing, lifelike dreams last night, either, which cheered him up and hinted he might be a lot saner and safer than he'd feared.

As he plodded into the kitchen, he paused next to the table, picked up the bottle of sleeping pills, and said "thank you" to it before setting it down. He could see a long future between himself and the pills, but if it kept the crazy dreams at bay, it would be worth it.

He opened the porch screen door and stuck his head out to take a look around. The sun had been exceptionally bright, but now the sky was darkening with the rapid arrival of storm clouds. He hoped the power wouldn't get knocked out again and hurried back into the kitchen to make breakfast before the storm arrived. In Ben's sudden haste to get started, he left the screen door unlatched.

The storm didn't pick up until after his breakfast was finished. What had begun as a gentle rain escalated quickly into a full-blown thunderstorm, and the cabin's lights flickered again.

With a groan, Ben resigned himself to the inevitability of losing power. He wasn't sure what he was going to do to pass the powerless time, but the one thing he'd ruled out was attempting to put another puzzle together. He didn't understand what had really happened with the last one, but there was a lingering, unexplained creepiness whenever he so much as looked at the box.

With an ear-splitting crack, lightning moved across the sky and touched down on the power transformer responsible for keeping the few cabins throughout the area lit up. He heard it pop and thought he could almost smell it sizzling as the cabin plunged into darkness. He wasn't surprised by the power outage but was still disappointed by this unfortunate turn of events. Although it was still relatively early in the morning, and it was now almost black as midnight.

Ben stepped into the enclosed porch. The storm pelted the lake with the vigor of someone plotting revenge, and he wondered what it was like to be a fish at that exact moment. Ominous, dark clouds filled an equally unfriendly sky, leaving him unable to see anything more than vague shapes between lightning strikes. When the lightning flashed, however, it lit up the surrounding area like the rays of the sun.

Contemplating how hot those flashes were left him grateful they'd only taken out the transformer instead of touching down on top of the cabin. It didn't take much imaginative thought to jump to the conclusion that if that happened, he would be fried alive.

The wind whipped up into a frenzy as the storm continued to rage on, knocking the screen doors loose and causing them to bang with fury inside of the door frames. He re-latched each of them twice before giving up; the power of the wind was simply too strong for a feeble little eye hook lock. The disquieting thought hit him that the same locks were intended to keep intruders out. If they couldn't stave off the wind, how could they hope to keep someone out who made it their intention to enter?

Pondering over this perplexing problem made him decide it was probably best to forget all about it. People had been employing such locks for decades, and they must have maintained at least a reasonably high success rate or they would've been phased out by now. These platitudes brought some peace to his mind. If he was being honest with himself, Ben was still bothered by the weakness of the locks, but he knew there wasn't a whole lot he could do about it.

Storms of this nature typically raged hard for a little while but also moved on just as fast as they had settled in. Due to this, he spent quite a lot of time doing nothing other than expecting the inclement weather to leave momentarily. After about ninety minutes of inaction, he grew to accept the fact that it wasn't going to vacate the area any time soon.

This left Ben as agitated as a chained-up dog in heat. With nothing else to do for entertainment, he decided to sit back and let the storm itself put on a show. He moved his chair to get the best possible view of the torrential rain and lightning as it hit the lake.

He sat and watched Mother Nature's show with varying levels of interest for several hours. At times, the sky lit up brilliantly, making him captivated and frightened by it. At other moments, the rain and wind looked like they would drone on forever. In both of these instances, he failed to remember his previous aversion to storms; for months, rain had elicited a PTSD response, but now, he enjoyed himself.

A new form of blackness unexpectedly fell over the lake, and it was not the kind that came from a darkened sky. It looked tangible, like it was an actual, living form of darkness. The idea seemed absurd, but his eyes continued to report to his brain that there was something hovering mere inches over the lake.

Ben couldn't make it out, but he could almost sense its presence. Whatever it was, it was immensely imposing and enormously large, and yet somehow empty. As he flipped the mental pages of his memory banks for something that could explain the disturbing imagery, the dark shape became even larger.

Is that the formation of a funnel cloud?

This thought grabbed his imagination, and it ballooned into fear for there was nowhere safe to go if a tornado was about to unleash its fury across the lake.

It would probably be a worthless endeavor, but Ben became resolved to at least put on a pair of shoes in an attempt at preparing for the possibility of the storm becoming disastrous. He bolted from the porch and pulled on his black and white Converse. He also grabbed a thin jacket while looking around the cabin in the hopes of being struck by some inspiration.

He had no idea what to do in the event of a tornado and knew there were no emergency supplies in the cabin. The only thing Ben could think of was to hide in the bathroom; but it was so freakishly small, and it also had a window, meaning it wouldn't provide safe harbor, either. In the end, he determined he'd rather face his doom, if it was coming, than be cowering before it when the tornado hit. He went back out to the porch, sat in his chair, and lit a cigarette.

His cigarette butt had burned down to the halfway point when the formation over the lake began to change. His jaw went slack, and his mouth became so dry that there was no longer enough saliva left to hold the cigarette up. It fell unnoticed from his lips, becoming extinguished in a gust of wind that hit the abandoned nicotine before it could touch the ground.

The dark clouds had formed into the blackened semblance of a monstrously large human skeleton. It flew toward him rapidly with its gargantuan mouth letting out an ear-splitting roar. Ben froze for a second and his bowels unclenched, filling his boxer shorts with the proof of his fear. The closer the cloud skeleton came, the larger it looked, until he was certain it would obliterate the cabin by merely touching it. The horrifying apparition's screams increased in their intensity, and Ben's ears shook as little pools of blood gathered in his eardrums before leaking on his shoulders.

He reflexively put his hands over his ears and fell to his knees, where he rocked back and forth. Every other item inside the enclosed porch swirled around him, no longer content to sit on the ground. The measure of wind that whipped past his body was surely as strong as an actual tornado would have been, and yet somehow, he managed to stay on his knees.

The cloud face hovered less than ten feet from the backdoor, and he could make out every twisted tooth in its mouth as it continued to roar at him. He knew this was going to be the last moment of his life, and Ben chose once again to face his destroyer as opposed to hiding.

With a monumental level of willpower, he held his head up high and dared to stare into the murderous eye sockets of his impending death. At the last possible second, he could no longer withstand the mixture of wind, noise, and overwhelming fear, so he lowered himself into a ball and prayed for a miracle.

The blackness of the clouds consumed the porch while the skeleton wrapped itself around him. It let out another roar, this one even higher pitched than the last, and descended upon Ben's shaking frame. A ghastly mixture of coldness and despair enveloped him before everything went completely still.

After a brief period of nothingness, he dared to raise his head. What he saw left him bewildered. It was a bright, sunny day, and every single piece of porch furniture was in the exact same place it had been a few moments before. With shaky knees, Ben stood up and looked out at the calm lake. It was then he figured out something was still terribly wrong. He couldn't hear anything. His hands quickly darted up to his ears and found them soaked in blood.

CHAPTER SIXTEEN

Ben noticed a slight ringing sound. He was initially relieved but then realized the sound was coming from inside his own head. He tried speaking aloud, but the only response was a strange distortion of the incessant ringing.

Fear flooded his body. What was he going to do? He was hundreds of miles from a hospital and couldn't stop thinking about the living cloud that had ripped his hearing away. Most of the other unusual encounters since his first night at the cabin had dissipated, but this particular incident was etched deeply into his psyche.

Did that really happen or am I flat out going insane? None of this makes any sense, but I had to lose my hearing somehow, right?

Terror and hopelessness made it impossible to keep his tears at bay. The entire situation was made even worse when he realized he couldn't hear his own sobbing.

Ben's tears stopped as his thinking began to clear. It was obvious that sitting here drowning in his sorrow wasn't going to help. The hospital might be far away, but it was the best chance he had at getting help or some type of rational explanation for his hearing loss. Hesitating no more, he left the cabin in such a rush that he didn't bother to lock the door.

The battered Honda Civic flew down the wooded path. The car followed the same route to the main road he'd traversed countless time, but when it made the final turn, the paved highway wasn't there.

"What the..."

Although he couldn't hear the sound of his voice, the distorted ringing peaked up in volume in conjunction with his words. Ben spun the car around and drove back down the path toward the cabin, thinking that perhaps he'd missed the correct turn.

The dirt path from the road to the cabin was less than three minutes long, but he traveled across it over and over again for more than an hour without finding a way out of the woods. Finally, he pulled the car back in front of the cabin and slammed the driver's side door. The entire car shook with the force of his anger.

He leaped up the three small steps that led to the cabin and ran inside screaming.

"What do you want from me?"

No response broke through the silence. His ears turned red and he was ready to fight someone. At this point, any type of sparring partner or punching bag would do as long as he could get out some of his pent-up frustration.

While stalking around the living room, Ben's eyes glanced across the table. He immediately did a double-take. Lying there was the perfectly formed puzzle of the Golden Gate Bridge. He flew to its side to definitively confirm what his eyes had reported.

Both his fists rained down on either side of the puzzle, making the table shake. The puzzle itself stayed intact in a show of defiance to his will. With his level of anger rising, he punched the middle of it. The puzzle refused to break apart as his barely healed knuckles were ripped asunder.

Ben unleashed such a torrent of dissatisfaction and terror that his right hand soon sang the discordant tune of painful, broken bones. He finally stopped the brutally ineffective onslaught and dejectedly lowered himself into a kitchen chair. Blood dripped onto the puzzle, but it did not appear on the pieces. Instead, the crimson liquid fell into the ocean and was washed away in a gentle wave.

Ben lifted his head and looked distrustfully toward the puzzle. He caught a glimpse of a figure standing on the bridge. After a slight hesitation, he drew closer and recognized the figure as himself.

His doppelganger stood dangerously close to the edge, looking mournfully down toward the water. It didn't happen instantly, but Ben put two and two together and figured out that his puzzle self was contemplating suicide. He wondered what would happen in the real world if his doppelganger jumped into the water.

He begged and pleaded with his duplicate to step back from the edge. The version of Ben inside the puzzle didn't appear to hear him, but it also didn't jump.

Maybe there's still a chance to save him.

Ben had a faint memory of being able to enter the puzzle. He'd almost fallen into the water then, but he thought he might be able to lower himself onto the bridge this time. Aware of how insane this idea was, he reached his hand toward the puzzle version of the Golden Gate Bridge.

Ben anticipated crisp, ocean air, but his fingers collided with the cardboard pieces of the puzzle. Frowning, he pulled his hand back. Maybe he was powerless to do anything before a jump had taken place? That thought left his blood cold, but he didn't have any alternative ideas.

He pushed back on the kitchen chair and stood up. He couldn't believe what he was thinking or what he'd just attempted to do. The entire thing was as absurd as his sudden hearing loss and his failed attempt at leaving the woods.

Ben might not have had any concrete answers, but he was damn certain jumping to supernatural conclusions wasn't going to help him maintain his dwindling sanity. He needed to think everything over very carefully and make some type of decision. To do that, he needed to keep his strength up.

Ben didn't have much of an appetite, but he still managed to choke down some food. While washing up, he was gripped by sorrow because he couldn't hear the water running. Little things he'd taken for granted now seemed so monumental. Ben paused long enough to mourn some of the other things he might never hear again.

Before his mind could go too far down an oppressively dark road, he forced himself to focus on finding a solution. He knew that getting lost in despair was a luxury he couldn't afford.

Ben had always been good at hiking, both from a physical standpoint and due to his impeccable sense of direction. *Maybe whatever caused the car to get lost wouldn't have the same effect on me alone?* With this in mind, he walked back to the front door and twisted the knob.

Nothing happened. His hand slipped across the knob like it was covered in warm butter when he made a second attempt. A vague recollection of something similar having already happened came over him, and Ben's sense of dread increased.

After a perceptible pause, his hand renewed its efforts but was met with the exact same results as the previous two attempts. Irritation mounted yet again. The whining and distortion in his ears went haywire, and he dropped to his knees in pain. The sensation was mercifully brief, and soon he got back up while muttering unheard curse words.

Ben tried everything he could think of to get the door open. He pushed it, kicked it, ran into it, twisted it with a towel covering the knob, yelled at it, and banged against it countless times. None of these methods worked, and he was left despondent and drenched in sweat.

None of this makes any sense.

The only possibility was so absurd he refused to accept it. After all, how could he believe that something supernatural was behind every odd occurrence from the past couple of weeks?

With nothing better to do, he went back to the kitchen table and sat down with a thud. He desperately wanted to avoid it, but Ben knew he must keep tabs on what his puzzle doppelganger was up to.

He steeled himself before fretfully glancing at the source of his current misery. Every hair on his body stood up. The version of himself that was contained within the puzzle was right at the edge of the bridge, apparently preparing to jump. Ben tried again to put his hand into the puzzle but was met with the same cardboard resistance from earlier.

Lacking any other solutions, he tried dismantling the puzzle. Rather than hitting it this time, his shaky fingers tried to pull it apart. The pieces wouldn't budge.

Every second he wasted trying to pry the pieces apart allowed his doppelganger to move closer to the jumping point. Finally, Ben's puzzle self glanced up with the strangest look of despair, peace, and smugness before walking off the edge of the bridge. Unlike other suicides, he hadn't jumped; he simply started walking in a straight line until there was nothing left to support his weight.

Fear gripped his heart as Ben watched himself fall through the air. The same crisp air somehow swirled around his physical body. He couldn't hear anything aside from an ever-present whining distortion, yet it also seemed like he could somehow hear the rush of the wind. As his cardboard self entered the water, it looked at him and flashed an evil grin.

Breathtaking cold and stabbing pain wracked his body. He fell to the ground and writhed on the cabin's hardwood floor. Water seeped out of his clothing. His lungs withstood the immense pressure of being crushed inside of a steel vise. Ben couldn't breathe, see, or hear; his entire body experienced all the sensations that accompany being submerged in the ocean.

His vital organs slowed their productivity, and Ben was left with the horrifying sensation of crawling toward a black hole. He was still lying on the cabin floor but was no longer physically connected to the hardness of the ground beneath him. In its place was the harshness of the water, along with the strong current that was intent on dragging him to a watery grave.

His body went numb, and his brain received numerous mixed signals from the disorientation of not being able to hear anything. The water pressure upon his eardrums and lungs was beyond anything he'd ever encountered before. The air around him became steadily darker until all he could see were muted globs of light. Ben's last cogent thought was *this must be what dying feels like.* It was far too difficult to try to swim, so he ceased struggling and gave his body over to the current while saying goodbye to his life.

Ben drifted deeper into the water with an almost graceful ease as his motions came to a halt. Peacefulness stole over him, and he derived comfort from the thought that he would no longer be best friends with mental anguish. In this state of drifting, he didn't observe the telltale fin headed straight toward him that would have otherwise sent his pulse skyrocketing.

The great white shark broke through his reverie when it furiously headbutted him. He exhaled for the first time in more than a minute and water refilled his lungs. Adrenaline inundated his brain and somehow thawed his limbs as he sputtered and struggled.

Ben's frantic motions enraged the shark, which swam with ease toward its intended victim. Crossing the distance in less than two heartbeats, the shark's massive mouth clamped down upon Ben's frigid right side. The pain of his body being severed in two sent him into shock. Blood gushed forth into the ocean, staining it temporarily red.

CHAPTER
SEVENTEEN

A huge gasp shook his chest. He coughed violently and spit out salt water on to the red ocean that had flooded the living room floor. He was astounded to discover that he was no longer struggling to stay afloat in the ocean.

There was water and blood all around him, and his flesh was blue-tinged and covered with goosebumps. It didn't make any sense, nor could he come up with a rational explanation for somehow surviving a direct attack from a great white shark. Still, he understood that his time in the puzzle definitely wasn't a delusion.

As soon as his fingers thawed out enough to work, Ben grabbed the right side of his shirt, lifted it, and almost fainted at the massive quantity of partially congealed blood. A closer look revealed no evidence of any actual wounds.

The entire experience defied all logic, but so did a lot of things recently. His mind quickly latched on to thoughts of the supernatural again. This time, he was a little more willing to consider such an absurd possibility.

Kyra popped into his mind as soon as he conceded that something supernatural might be afoot. It surprised him that he hadn't been thinking about her nearly as much as usual during the past several days. He wondered if that was due to the influence of whatever was impacting his daily life. A horrible realization came over Ben, and it begged a vital question: *Could Kyra be involved?*

He couldn't imagine she would put him through something like this. Then again, she might be filled with righteous anger over her untimely death. Before his thoughts could wander to the events behind her accident, Ben forced himself to stop being ridiculous and focus instead on the meager details he knew about supernatural phenomena throughout history.

Nothing he'd ever read about or seen in a movie was anything like this. *Perhaps each spirit has just as unique of a personality as every living human?*

This idea didn't bring him any comfort, for with it came the knowledge that some people were evil for the sake of being evil. There didn't have to be a reason at all; it could simply be that there was someone out there who thought it was fun to mess with him, and maybe even break him. Ben's trembling jaw tried unsuccessfully to bolster itself against whomever or whatever might be looking at him.

How can I trust what I'm feeling and seeing? For all I know, I've gone crazy like Mom.

Maybe there was no water around him; perhaps there had never even been a puzzle. There was no way to know for sure, nothing with which to gauge his sanity against.

Ben was desperate and hopelessly confused. The shark attack wounds might not have become visible on his body, but all his organs kept claiming they'd been separated and ground into little pieces by humongous knives. After several failed attempts, he managed to rise up into a sitting position. The pain receptors in his body applauded his accomplishment with an overwhelming enormity of pain. Unable to withstand the latest assault, he blacked out.

The sun finished crossing the sky and set over the lake as his torpid stupor raged on. No dreams or thoughts entered or exited his frame; he was in a blank state from which his eroding mind did not wish to wake.

A blackness that didn't originate from the setting of the sun entered the cabin. Three cloudy, indistinct shapes filled the room. The largest shape looked down upon him with disgust. They made no noises, but the cabin itself creaked in terror.

Cabin Green had known many different experiences during its more than one-hundred-year history, and something deep within the knots of its wood told it that these shapes were bad news. The wood itself tried in vain to scream out to the sleeping man who had frequented it for so many years without causing any damage.

The blackness paused like it could read the cabin's thoughts before a harsh, evil cackle broke the stillness. There was no discernable face or mouth from which the sound emanated, but this didn't stop the discordant noise from being extraordinarily loud and long. No one but the darkness and the cabin itself heard anything, though, and the darkness seemed to know and thrive upon this knowledge.

The darkness lowered its massive fog-like shape toward Ben and caressed his body like a lover. It whispered unintelligible words into his wasted ears, and against all laws of reality, he began to stir.

What was that?

"Yes," it hissed in a voice that had no semblance of humanity. "Fall into me."

Ben's body flipped over, ignoring the internal screams of pain, until he was lying flat on his back. His eyes were still closed against the real world, but his arms rose as if to return a comforting embrace.

The darkness swooped down and lifted his body several feet into the air. Ben's arms wrapped around nothingness, but they insisted they'd found something solid to hold onto. Tears streamed out of the corners of his eyes as his ears re-opened. He could hear the mutterings of the darkness, and what it said was horrifying. The disembodied voice insisted, "It was your fault."

He screamed "No!" but his protests were silenced by a cold wisp of air that muzzled his mouth.

"Accept it!" the darkness yelled back.

His head shook back and forth so vigorously that it looked like it could pop off at any second. With a loud, trembling sound of exasperation, he was thrown to the floor like a discarded toy. His head cracked against the ground with a sickening thud.

CHAPTER EIGHTEEN

Eight Years Ago

Ben sorted through his mail, discarding the junk and looking for anything worth the effort of opening. The Banks Psychiatric Care logo was emblazoned upon one of the envelopes. The shock of being contacted by his mother made the world tilt a little to the left. Then it hit him like a bucket of cold water

What if this isn't from her? Oh, please no. She didn't...

Leaving the thought unfinished, he tore the letter free, yanked it open, and immediately scanned to the bottom. A tidal wave of relief accompanied the mere act of seeing his mother's handwritten name. Realizing that he was gripping the counter, Ben decided to sit down at the kitchen table before seeing what had made her finally respond to his numerous visitation attempts.

Benjamin,

You have no idea how difficult it's been to restrain myself from jumping at the chance to see you. I know that makes no sense; you've been here several times now since the last time we spoke. It breaks my heart to say 'no' when you come, but you need to know I'm doing it to protect you.

There's no way to explain everything I know. Even if I did, you probably wouldn't believe me. I wouldn't believe me either, if I didn't know that it's the truth. All I can say, and I pray that you'll listen, is that you need to stay far away from him. Please do this for me, Ben.

If I could have told you this in person, I would have. He taught me the last time he can see and hear everything we say to each other, though. I can't take that risk.

Please, son. Stay away from him. And for your own good, stay away from me. He won't hurt you if you stay away from both of us.

Don't blame your father. He was a good man once. It's <u>not</u> his fault he stopped being that person.

I love you,
Mom

PS – Burn this letter. Tell no one.

"What the fuck?" he said, while turning the letter over in his hands. *You're right, Mom, this doesn't make any sense at all.* In that moment, Ben understood that despite his mother's protestations, she was truly insane. *There's no other way to explain this letter. I'm sorry, Mom.*

He shoved the letter back into the envelope and put it in a filing cabinet. The file folder in question, labeled 'Mom,' contained all the documentation he'd collected about the night she'd disappeared.

Dad is nuts, and he most definitely is at fault for his actions, but I'm away from him. He can't hurt me anymore.

For one faltering second, Ben wondered if she meant someone else. This trail didn't lead him anywhere, so he ultimately wrote it off. He also made the decision to skip his next scheduled visitation attempt. He reasoned that giving her a few more months, or even a year, might help her gain the clarity and psychiatric help she needed to stop cowering at the thought of her ex-husband.

He can't hurt you anymore, Mom.

CHAPTER NINETEEN

Present Day

Cobwebs cluttered Ben's mind, and all his limbs ached with the strain of having run a sleeping marathon. The distorted ringing had disappeared from his ears. He missed it for a second, thinking he would now have no noises at all to accompany him. While these thoughts crossed his mind, he popped his back and heard the familiar cracking sound of his bones. Startled, his body stiffened in response before hope lit up his face.

"Hello!"

The most wonderful sound he'd ever encountered vibrated through his ears and he got up much too fast in his excitement. Dizziness left him no choice but to brace himself against the wall until little white spots stopped dancing in front of his eyes. Relief calmed his mind as he spoke again and heard each word.

Ben had little to no memories of the previous night. He was again unsure why he'd greeted a new day from the uncomfortable living room floor. Tiny traces of matted blood in his hair provided another shock. Every muscle ached and grogginess filled his mind and limbs. Overall, though, he seemed okay.

He glanced at the kitchen table and caught himself recoiling for no discernable reason. There was nothing there except for the salt and pepper shakers that were mandatory for all his hot food consumption. He saw a flash in his mind's eye of the puzzle, along with one of himself jumping off the Golden Gate Bridge. It shook him up a bit, but he pushed it away, writing it off as the remnants of a bad dream.

With his hearing restored, he wanted to listen to music for the first time since arriving at the cabin. He pulled his iPhone and ear buds from his backpack and selected Stabbing Westward. They were one of his favorite bands, but they also fed into his depression over the loss of Kyra.

While making breakfast, Ben listened to '*Waking Up Beside You*' repeatedly, and his thoughts lingered over the message contained within the song. He missed any number of the daily pleasures that being with Kyra had given to him. What he grieved for most of all was the single thing he'd been most looking forward to about married life; the opportunity to wake up next to her every single day.

A deep depression crept over him as breakfast sizzled in the frying pan. He didn't have the energy to fight, so it overtook him with ease. Ben picked at his breakfast without ingesting most of it.

He stumbled out to the porch and sat down heavily with the weight of the world pushing him into the chair. Once his morning cigarette was extinguished, he let his head drop into his hands and sat there motionless for an extended time period. No tears escaped; his emotions were too deep and raw to allow for any type of release. Guilt besieged him, and he began to believe he'd taken the coward's way out by coming to the cabin.

Ben knew he'd been utterly useless to Kyra's family during their time of grief. He wondered if they could ever look past his selfishness and allow him a small place within their close-knit group. They represented so much of Kyra, and he wanted to hold on to that. Yet he wasn't suitable to be around anyone else.

Maybe I never will be again.

His thoughts shifted away from her family and landed on his friends. They had put up with a lot over the past few months, but many of them had drifted away before he came to the cabin. Would he be able to repair any of those relationships? Should he even attempt to?

Why hasn't anyone called or texted? It might be time to leave the cabin.

Memories jumped into place, and along with them came flashes of being incapable of leaving the day before. He hesitated but soon walked with a sense of purpose through the cabin toward the front door. The knob turned underneath his hand, and the door sprang to life. Relieved, he shut the door again, admonishing himself for having entertained such crazy thoughts. There was obviously nothing wrong with the door. He understood that people who were severely stressed or depressed would sometimes exhibit delusional behavior. This rang true, which left him convinced he'd been experiencing something similar.

The entire idea of a door refusing to open or a puzzle making him creeped out was preposterous, perhaps even more so than the ultra-delusional thoughts he slightly remembered about ghosts and spirits.

I need to stop letting my imagination run so wild.

Exhausted from the previous night's half-remembered events, he sat on the couch and ignored the old furniture's complaints. Ben knew he needed to gain some much-needed perspective on his depression and odd supernatural thoughts. With no conceivable alternatives, he decided to try meditating.

Kyra had taught him how to calm his mind and slip into a meditative state. It was difficult work at first, but he'd come to enjoy it. By the end of their first year together, he'd reached a state where he could let his mind go with his eyes still open. That peacefulness was shattered by Kyra's death, but he hoped he'd be able to recapture it now.

Find your center, find your center, find your...

Post-apocalyptic scenes flashed though his mind. He watched as people were herded into large structures like baseball stadiums and schools. He saw several small groups hidden in unexpected places such as underneath the tarp of a drained-out swimming pool. All the streets within view were utter chaos and surrounded by damage and destruction. There was no electricity, and from the screams he heard, it became apparent there was no clean water, either.

Struggling to leave these thoughts behind and focus on nothingness, Ben launched into a mental countdown. *One, two, three, four...*

It worked for about half a second. His inner eye was shocked from the calmness by the clack of guns being pulled and fired from all directions. The lack of hesitation informed him that someone nearby would murder him too without any remorse. Although his body was sitting on a couch in Cabin Green, he believed the gunshots were real. He dived to the ground to avoid being hit by a stray bullet. Everywhere he looked, Ben could see a war-torn landscape filled with signs of looting and violence.

He stumbled through the streets without any concrete sense of purpose until the cellphone he hadn't realized was with him rang in his pocket. He yanked it free and was stunned to see Kyra's name staring at him from the caller ID.

"Hello?"

The voice that responded wasn't Kyra's.

"It's your fault. All of it. You did this."

The line went dead. He stared at the phone as if it had bitten him. The accusatory words swirled around in his brain until they put down roots. He peered around at all the destruction and chaos, wondering if he could actually have been the one responsible for it. Before he could spend too much time contemplating this, the trancelike state shifted.

Ben looked down from his new vantage point located several thousand miles above the ground. He flew with ease and without wings or any manmade piece of machinery. The wind whipped through his hair and made ripples in the legs of his jeans. He was lighthearted and jubilant, as if he'd never had a care in the world.

The bluest sky he'd ever seen stretched out before him, broken only by the whitest, puffiest clouds. It was like being in a Bob Ross painting, and he cherished the sensation. This was one of his meditation safe places, and finding it brought his pulse back down to a normal level.

His lightheartedness and satisfaction didn't last long. Storm clouds appeared in the distance, and they threatened to ruin his moment of inner peace. Ben spun his body around in an attempt to fly away from the storm clouds, but they spun with him. Disturbed, he tried spinning in every possible direction until he'd spun three-hundred-sixty degrees around, back all the way to where he'd started.

No matter what he did or which way he turned, the dark clouds managed to keep following him. The most bizarre thing of all was that the clouds were always straight ahead. If he looked to his left and right, he could see nothing but perfect blue skies.

Each time Ben shifted course toward the peaceful skies, the storm clouds filled the new space. It made no sense, but he soon grasped the fact that there was nothing he could do to keep from flying into the storm.

Resigned to his fate, Ben stopped attempting to change his course. The air pushed him toward the blackened sky. As he approached it, a surge of electricity zapped through his body, causing every hair to stand straight up. He detected a hint of copper on his tongue, and ozone and petrichor filled the air.

Ben spotted a massive, blackened thunderhead closing in. Forgetting the lesson he'd learned a few minutes earlier, he struggled to push away from this new threat. His movements propelled him forward with greater speed, and he melted into the cloud faster than he could blink.

The dark cloud brushed over his skin. It was unlike any other feeling on Earth. It wasn't substantial at all, and yet it somehow noticeably changed his body temperature and left him shivering. Ben assumed he would pass through the thunderhead as quickly as he'd approached it, but the cloud's movements came to a halt when he reached the center.

The cloud let loose a horrifying whooshing sound and rain poured forth from its frame. At this altitude, the rain wasn't merely freezing; it also came in drops bigger than his head and soaked him instantly.

It was black as midnight, and Ben's body soon informed him it was being waterboarded. His breathing became labored, followed shortly by the distinct lethargy and numbness of hypothermia. Something about this seemed familiar, although he couldn't figure out why.

Without any warning, he fell through the cloud. Ben tried to regain the power of flight, but his body refused to cooperate. In desperation, his arms flailed out, attempting to find anything that could stop his downward trajectory. His hands closed through the clouds and found nothing solid enough to save his life.

The velocity of his unwelcome descent picked up steam as he fell. Soon, the topography beneath him turned into discernable land masses. Wind rushed through his ears and smacked him around as his brain struggled to deal with the knowledge of his impending doom.

At least it should be more or less instantaneous.

Less than ninety seconds of falling had enabled Ben to travel from the upper reaches of the atmosphere to the ground. His body crashed down with so much force that every bone broke, each organ ruptured, and parts of his body were instantly liquefied.

Somehow, he lived through the hellish experience, but he had zero gratitude for his misfortune. Every nerve ending in his body screamed out in rage, yet there was nothing he could do to escape from the torment. He was pummeled again and again by waves of pain, each one progressively worse than the last. Ben cried out for an end to his suffering, but no one was around to listen to his complaints.

Although he no longer had a functional body, he could still spin his head around with ease. There was a thick forest of tall, untamed trees in every direction. However, the growth of the forest became stunted the closer it got to him, until it petered out into a mere copse of bushes. Trees in the distance were verdant, but the brilliant sunshine and lack of rain had scorched the area beneath him. The dry, brittle, brownish appearance reminded him of unhealthy wheat long past its 'best if harvested by' date.

One, two, three, four, five. One, two, three, four, five.

He focused on his counting exercises, attempting to regain control of the meditation session. When this failed, Ben reached out to each part of his body. This was a process he'd done countless times before, starting at his toes.

No matter how hard he concentrated, his toes weren't responsive. Panicked, he kept trying to move up his body, hoping to connect with anything. All his efforts fell flat until he reached his head. He had to face a horrible truth: his body had turned into a wasteland, making him incapable of movement.

Excruciatingly long hours passed, and the sun set to work frying some of the remaining portions of his skin. He could smell his flesh burning. It didn't take long for vultures to start circling overhead, waiting for Ben to finish dying. The large birds appeared confused by his semi-alive state because this didn't mesh with everything else they were seeing and smelling.

What seemed like hours of burn-induced pain passed before the lead vulture did a surface check. The large shadow swooped ever closer until it reached his entrails. The carrion bird sniffed toward them, paused, cocked its head, and looked him straight in the eyes.

Oh, my fucking God, he's going to eat me. He's going to eat me!

A soul-shattering sound passed through its beak, then the scavenger shot back up into the sky. Ben exhaled through trembling lips, certain his breathing head had persuaded the large birds of prey to look elsewhere for food.

Sadly, he didn't know much about vultures. He didn't understand they weren't going to give up on him until they ripped apart his flesh, adding his unwilling offering into their digestive systems. They were nature's garbagemen and took their disposal job very seriously.

The carrion leader stayed close by and descended multiple times to check on him before flying away after determining that Ben still lived. Ben's screaming and most of the pain had passed away hours ago. His weary eyes only stayed because he feared the birds would swoop down upon him and pick him apart as soon as he fell asleep. Giving into that fate might have made the most sense given his current situation. Like most people, though, he found himself holding on to the last shreds of his life with a voracity he hadn't known could still exist in his world.

Despite Ben's best efforts, he reached a point where he could no longer keep his eyes open. After several false starts, his lids dropped shut with the finality of sleep, leaving him unaware of everything outside his dreams.

The lead vulture picked up on the change almost instantly. With a piercing cry that somehow did not separate Ben from sleep, all three birds swooped toward him. The leader had first pick and went straight for his head. This was the piece that had troubled the bird for so long. It wanted to be the one to make sure the head was disposed of.

While the other buzzards made quick work of his salvageable body parts, the leader pecked frantically at his right eyelid. This activity woke Ben up, but he was paralyzed and couldn't make any movements or sounds.

The bird's massive beak hammered down into his weak flesh a couple of times before finding the juicy treasure it sought. Ben's eye was violently ripped from its socket. The tenacious vulture slurped the eye into its mouth, then lifted its neck toward the sky to hasten the eye's departure down its throat.

The other vultures stopped dining for a second and bore witness to the spectacle, cackling their approval in a horrifying cacophony. Ben stayed connected to his eye after its forcible eviction from his body. Against his will, he saw everything through it, along with feeling the associated sensations of his eyeball sliding down the bird's throat and into its digestive tract.

CHAPTER TWENTY

The distant sound of chimes from the iPhone's alarm released Ben from his nightmare meditation. He bolted up from the ground where he'd fallen, covered in sweat that dripped from his entire body. Several deep breaths helped calm his erratic heart rate, but it still persisted at beating much faster than usual.

The ultra-realism of the meditation-induced hallucination left him unable to resist the urge to lift his hand up to his right eye. The eyelid was soaking wet, but Ben assumed it was just sweat.

What the hell was that? No more meditation for me.

He'd had a few surreal meditation experiences in the past, and it wasn't unheard of for him to dip into a nearly comatose state for a short time. However, nothing as crazy as this had ever happened before, and he had a hard time wrapping his brain around it. Ben grappled with an ever-growing fear of his own mind as he double-checked his phone's alarm.

How was that only thirty minutes? It felt like hours. It felt like days.

He hauled himself up onto the couch and sat still. Ben's uncertainty kept him rigid, but his body continued to calm down. Just as he was becoming lulled into the safety of everyday banality, he heard a sound that make his stomach clench.

There's no way.

The sound came again, accompanied by a deep scratching noise that echoed out of the kitchen. Rooted with fear, Ben's head swiveled to the right. His mouth hung agape as he once again made eye contact with the buzzard from his mind. He shut his eyes and reopened them several times, followed by rubbing them vigorously with the back of his hands. The bird of prey didn't disappear, but something else made itself known; he had streaks of blood on his hand.

No. That's not true. I can see out of my eyes, I didn't lose one.

This inner babble was intended to calm himself, but it had the exact opposite effect. The buzzard, sensing his prey was about to make a move, issued a piercing cry.

Ben realized his problems had somehow tripled as he jumped to his feet. The three vultures were here in the cabin, looking at him hungrily. His mental defense mechanisms screamed that the birds weren't there, but his feet didn't listen. Ben dashed toward the back door and bolted free of it, slamming the door in his wake.

His feet pounded the ground as the door flew open again behind him, releasing the three birds for the hunt. Ben's legs pumped harder than ever before, but it wasn't enough to outpace the fierce carrions. Tripping over a stick, he slammed to the ground.

The instinct to flee propelled him back into a crawling position, and he made it a few more feet before his skin went cold beneath the beating of the lead bird's wings. Out of options, he curled into a ball and shoved his face into the dirt in a last-ditch attempt to save his eyes. Each bird slammed into his back in quick succession but then disappeared. Trembling, he rocked on the ground for a long time before taking the risk of looking around.

No predators were within view, and he implored himself to believe it had all been some type of waking nightmare. Unsatisfied by this explanation but unwilling to admit the entire thing might have really happened, he returned to the cabin. The last thing he spotted before locking the barely attached screen door was a huge black feather lying just outside.

CHAPTER TWENTY-ONE

"Okay, thanks Mark. I will. Bye."

With a worried look on his face, Doug clicked the end call button on the iPhone's touchscreen.

Is there anything I could be forgetting? Did Ben tell me he was going to leave his phone turned off?

He had no recollection of anything like that. Even if that had been the plan, Doug would have insisted on at least getting a text after Ben arrived at the resort. No, the reality was that something must be wrong.

He'd contacted Mark and Stephen, along with a few acquaintances, and no one had heard anything from Ben since the day he'd left town. Some of them had also reached out with texts and voicemails of their own, but they were all met with radio silence.

This made zero sense. Yes, Ben could be shy and private, but he always kept his closest friend posted about his whereabouts, especially during road trips. Doug tried not to let himself get overly worried, but he had to face the fact that something might be seriously wrong.

Ryan reached out to Doug and firmly but lovingly grabbing his hands. "Still nothing?"

"Yeah. No one has heard from him. I'm getting really worried, Ryan."

Ryan considered whether or not to offer some words of reason or to simply placate his anxious husband. In his heart, he knew neither of these options was the right answer.

"Come sit with me," he said, while guiding Doug to the couch.

Their eyes met, and Ryan could see Doug was a few heartbeats away from crying. Doug's trepidation made Ryan realize his husband was probably right; something most likely had gone wrong. He didn't know Ben as well as Doug did, but the thought of something bad happening left him with a hitch in his throat.

"Okay, I admit it; I gave you terrible advice the other day. You know Ben better than anyone, so if you think something's wrong, that's something we need to honor and act upon. I'm happy to help. Let me call the resort, and we'll get this all figured out."

Doug looked relieved to have Ryan's full support and assistance. He nodded in agreement.

"Thank you, love. That means the world to me. Yes, if you could call the resort, I'm going to call the state police in each state he drove through. I've already searched Google for any accident news, but we know they don't report everything."

With tasks assigned, the two men headed into opposite rooms. Doug reached the headquarters of three state police branches, but none of them were helpful.

Ryan's luck wasn't any better. He dialed and listened to eight ring tones before reaching the resort's voicemail. The line disconnected before he could leave a message. This exact sequence happened at least twenty more times before Doug came to him with a pleading look in his eyes.

"I'm sorry, I can't seem to get through," Ryan said with a mixture of anger and confusion. "Hey, wait a minute. Have you checked the weather in Virginia Beach? Are they having storms? Maybe an extended power outage? That would certainly explain a lot."

Crestfallen, Doug said, "I checked. It's been dry, sunny, and unseasonably warm there for weeks. Whatever is going on has nothing to do with weather or a power outage."

The two shared a concerned look, and Ryan made it clear he'd keep trying until someone either picked up or the voicemail stopped hanging up on him. Doug went back to calling the headquarters of various state police branches from Michigan to Virginia.

Several fruitless hours later, they conceded defeat for the night. They went to bed almost immediately, but it took Doug a long time to fall asleep. His last waking thought centered on the notion that something was very, very wrong with Ben.

CHAPTER TWENTY-TWO

Ben examined his face in the bathroom mirror and saw blood smeared by his eye.

That's just from sticking my face into the dirt.

This didn't ring true, but he tried to deny what he already knew; the blood had been there when he'd come out of the meditation. But how could your eye bleed from something that took place in your mind?

He had no sane answer for this question and elected to put it away for another day. With a strange sensation coursing through his body, he removed his soiled clothes and took a shower. The unmelodious noises that had become his shower time soundtrack returned, but he did his best to ignore them.

Bathing got rid of the sweat and blood, and it was a lot easier to feign ignorance without any remaining evidence. By the time he'd put on fresh clothes and started warming up the stove for a quick meal, the entire incident had seeped away from his conscious mind.

He reached into the lower cabinet to grab a frying pan. What his hand connected with, though, was definitely not something meant for cooking. Stunned, Ben went down on his haunches to take a closer look. Upon seeing what he'd touched, his pale, gaunt face lost whatever minimal coloring it had obtained during the summer.

"That's n-not possible," he said, while backing away.

Ben's memories threw him almost five years into the past. Doug, Stephen, and Mark were helping him clean up the newly acquired cabin. Stephen worked in the bathroom, Mark washed the walls, and Ben set about the task of filling cracks with caulk. Doug startled them with his outburst from the kitchen.

"Holy crap, man! You guys are never going to believe this crazy shit. Get over here!"

All three of the men, each in their mid-twenties, joined Doug in the kitchen.

"What's up?" Mark asked before Doug could begin to offer an explanation.

Ben, who knew Doug better than the others, detected a hint of something disturbing beneath his long-term friend's grinning face. This put him on edge. What were they about to see? Did he really want to see it? Before Ben could finish unraveling this internal puzzle, Doug had reverently pulled a large, circular, silver tray out of the lower cabinet's bottom shelf.

"Whoa," Mark said, and it became clear that the resident jokester of the group didn't find anything funny at all about this macabre discovery.

There, on the silver plate, sat a fully cleaned cat skull. Even worse, the gruesome discovery was encircled by a mysterious white powder. A beat or two passed without any commentary before Mark recovered his infamous prankster persona.

"What's the powder? Cocaine? Score! Free cocaine!"

This was meant to be funny as opposed to being an actual suggestion. The guys had all experimented with minor drugs, but none of them had any desire to do cocaine.

"I don't like this," Ben mumbled.

The other guys either didn't hear or flat-out ignored Ben's protest in their rush to examine the skull. Before he could say anything else, Stephen picked the skull up and tested the sharpness of the deceased cat's teeth.

"Fuck!"

A canine tooth, combined with Stephen's carelessness, managed to cut open the thumb on his left hand. The wound wasn't deep, and there was hardly any blood spilled. Still, it was enough to give everyone's laughter a nervous tone.

"I don't think you should play with that anymore," Ben said in a louder tone.

"You may be right," Stephen retorted. "But it's not because some curse is on this place, if that's what you're thinking. The damn thing has sharp teeth, that's all."

"Yeah," Doug said. "I think the skull and, let's face it, the entire presentation is very weird, but let's not spin out of control here. This cabin was owned by an older guy who came here for years to hunt and take a break from corporate America. This must have been his idea of a sick joke because he's so not the type to get into anything hinky like voodoo or witchcraft."

Stephen said, "Exactly. Sure, this is a cabin in the middle of the woods, but that doesn't mean we've stumbled into a horror movie. There's not going to be any Kandarian demons or backwoods redneck zombie families coming for us. This is someone's idea of a sick joke, so let's just chuck it. Okay?"

All eyes turned toward Ben, and his face became hot. The others knew he enjoyed watching horror movies and could sometimes let his imagination run away to dark and spooky places. Not wanting to appear weak, he nodded his agreement.

Without any further discussion, the four cabin co-owners went outside to dispose of their bizarre housewarming gift. Ben was revolted by the skull's appearance, and it brought his beloved cat, Kali, to mind. It was with much relief that he watched Stephen toss the skull into the garbage can, followed by Doug throwing away the silver plate.

If they had talked about it later, each of the men would have learned they'd all felt odder than they wanted to acknowledge. Everyone, including Mark, was also surprised Mark didn't attempt any last-minute jokes about the powder. Somehow, they all intuitively understood this topic wasn't to be broached again, and that was precisely what they'd done. Ben had even managed to forget about the entire incident until uncovering the same display once again.

Now, the cat's empty eye sockets bored a hole through his forehead. The unpleasant taste of pennies filled the back of his throat. Ben braced himself for what he knew must come next; picking up the plate and disposing of it yet again. He tried twice to grab it before backing away at the last second. With his hands shaking, he finally managed to pick up the wretched thing and rushed it outside.

The skull, plate, and white powder were about to be tossed into the same garbage can as before when the skull moved and released a long, mournful meow. Ben dropped the plate like it had burned him. This wasn't merely a dead cat's skull meowing at him. No, this sounded exactly like his sixteen-year partner in crime, Kali, who had passed away two months after Kyra came into his life. Pain filled his eyes, but the clattering of the silver plate as it landed on the ground helped him refocus.

This living nightmare worsened as the skull and powder transformed into hundreds of writhing maggots. Their putrid, fat, white bodies wriggled all over the plate. A few of the more enterprising maggots managing to crawl onto the ground. In horror, Ben noted they were undulating in his direction.

"Shit!"

He jumped back so fast that he tripped over a stick and fell down. The accompanying adrenaline rush made it possible to temporarily tear his bulging eyes away from the platter. When he looked again, his surprised gasp could have carried half-a-mile to the next cabin. There was nothing there, not even a plate.

Did I imagine it?

This seemed crazy, but Ben preferred the idea of having a temporary moment of insanity over the alternative.

Two double-takes later, he turned back to the faded green cabin. The entry door was now completely adorned with dead ivy, and the interior seemed mustier than usual. He attempted several times to open the kitchen window in pursuit of fresh air, but it held fast. Frowning, he spotted the problem. Ivy also protruded from the exterior of the window, and a layer of mold covered the inside track.

With a slight tremble moving throughout his body, Ben sat down at the kitchen table to regroup. *Where the hell is all this ivy coming from? And now mold? Ugh.*

He reached for a pack of cigarettes with the certainty that smoking would help calm his nerves. He'd pondered off and on during the past couple of days about trying to quit, but the slender object currently balancing between two fingers seemed like his only friend in the entire world. Therefore, it was going to have to stick around for at least a little while longer.

After a long, leisurely smoke Ben went into the kitchen and stuck his head under the faucet for a quick drink of water. This was one habit of his that had really irritated Kyra. She would always ask, "Why don't you just grab a glass?"

He replied the same way each time: "There's no reason to dirty a glass for nothing more than a sip."

She'd issue her retort in the form of a quick, disapproving look, but within seconds, a smile would steal over her features and they'd embrace and share a kiss. It had become so engrained into their routine that it almost felt like a miniature play they acted out in the midst of their everyday life.

He missed little stuff like that most of all. He wondered if it would have stayed so cute after marriage or if it would've ended up becoming one of those little unraveling threads that turned into an actual argument. Ben assumed they would've either maintained their civility or he would have given up on the little quirk and taken to drinking from an actual glass. Now he'd never know for sure.

As always, allowing his mind to veer to Kyra caused a whirlwind of emotions. Ben choked back the tears that threatened to spill down his cheeks. Grief stained his pale, gaunt face, leaving him with harsh black circles under his eyes. None of his tears had done much to help him with the task of moving on, though. Maybe it was time to stop crying.

Ben mustered up all his willpower and pushed the urge away. He didn't know if tears would actually be helpful in terms of getting over the loss of Kyra, but one thing was certain; they weren't going to help him figure out what had really been happening since he entered the cabin a couple weeks ago.

He opened a heavy drawer, ignoring its squeaks of protest. Even here in the cabin with all its bare necessity charm, they'd still managed to cobble together the stereotypical junk drawer that resides within millions of homes. He pushed his hands through the mess. An old notepad and a black ink pen were the fruits of his labor. Ben shoved everything else back into its disorganized placement and shut the drawer carefully.

With the notebook and pen in hand, he walked over to the kitchen table and sat down. It was time to make a list of everything he could remember. He brimmed with newfound confidence.

Getting everything on paper has to unveil any recent patterns.

Ben started with the vague memories of his meditation session from a few hours ago. The only part that really stood out to him was losing an eye, but he also had a faint recollection of real blood on his hand and face after the alarm went off. He frowned down at the newly-written details. Why was it so difficult to be certain of memories from less than two hours ago?

The old black ink pen made an audible scratching sound as it rolled its ink onto the stark whiteness of the paper. Ben struggled in a valiant attempt to dredge up anything else. Fragments that may have been real or merely something from a dream flitted through his mind. He wrote them down anyway. Next, he turned his attention to the mystery of the puzzle box on the mantel.

Why does it bother me so much?

He briefly contemplated the irony of being afraid of one puzzle while trying so hard to piece another one together. It took an extended stretch of concentration, but he finally pulled forth a memory. Ben shuddered as he wrote down the scant details that had come back to him.

His mind flashed back to the weirdest thing yet. He couldn't quantify its placement in his memories, but Ben saw mountains of bones being buried on what appeared to be the island in the lake. After writing it down, he paused and looked back at his scattered list.

1. Bad meditation, lost eye, blood on hand/face after?

2. Something sent me outside?

3. Strong storm, knocked off my feet.

4. Woods, car, couldn't drive out?

5. Puzzle is creepy, someone jumped, freezing cold.

6. Huge pile of bones, buried on the island?

The nearly indecipherable handwriting was his own, but it all looked like absolute gibberish. Ben questioned the entire exercise. How could any of the things on the notepad have any basis in reality? Even if they did, what was he suggesting by thinking these fragmented events might be related?

The rational part of his mind screamed at him to give up the ghosts and admit that bad dreams and an overactive imagination were the true root of his fear. Another part of his brain argued that there were so many unknown things in the world. Wouldn't it be ridiculous to discount his possible experiences with such haste?

The internal debate raged on. By the time he tired of it, there weren't any more memories willing to surface. Discouraged, he let his head drop into his hands and ran his fingers through his hair, twisting and pulling at a few different strands.

The idea of sleep made Ben nervous, but an overwhelming exhaustion crept over his limbs. He remembered to grab a sleeping pill to help keep his mind's wild nocturnal activities at bay. Two hours of deep sleep passed without incident; no dreams and no unexpected wakefulness came for him.

His arms stretched across the mattress while the rest of his body and mind slumbered on. Instinctively, he knew someone else's weight had been added to the bed. Ben's arms sought out a specific frame, and they weren't disappointed. Kyra was here again, and she melted against him without any hesitation.

Her warmth brought his sleeping body temperature back up to a waking range. He smiled in his sleep and nuzzled the back of her neck. She fit against him more perfectly than he'd remembered, and he reveled in the delicious aroma of her perfume.

In his sleeping state, there was no such thing as a rational mind. Ben's emotions and sense of longing ruled his actions. Without waking up, his desire for her grew until she noticed it against her leg.

Kyra's body turned toward him and whispered into his left ear, "You must keep your eyes closed if we're to do this."

He enthusiastically nodded his agreement, and she reached down to his boxer shorts and pulled them free of his body. Unencumbered, his interest in her became even more readily apparent. The sudden enormity of his interest brought a playful giggle to her lips.

Kyra rolled over onto her back and used her hands to communicate this change to his sightless body. Ben needed no further encouragement and climbed on top of her. His need was so strong that foreplay didn't enter his mind. She didn't seem to mind, and in fact encouraged him to move things along at a quick pace.

After a microsecond of hesitation, Ben dove deep inside of Kyra with a bit more force than usual. She grabbed his back and clawed at it while moaning into his ear on each downward thrust.

With great abandon, he plunged on, ever deeper and harder. Kyra reacted with an almost reckless level of noise while she scratched deep enough to leave red droplets all over his back and neck. He couldn't have cared any less in that moment about sustaining any physical damage, nor could he have been any happier at her rapturous reaction.

A huge release ripped through Ben's body, leaving him shuddering in pleasure. She accompanied him with a simultaneous orgasm. Her body bucked underneath his, then shook from aftershocks until she went still, covered in sweat and ready for rest.

Not wanting their time together to end, he waited a while before he slid out of her, rolled to his side, and took her into his arms. He fell asleep while inhaling the scent of her hair.

* * * * *

Ben was jarred awake by a disorienting sound. It took a few beats for his sleep-addled brain to recognize the discordant beeping of the living room smoke detector. In fear, he hopped out of bed and ran into the main portion of the cabin.

The notebook he'd written his list on was consumed by flames. Burning paper and smoke lashed out with the apparent intention of draining the cabin's supply of fresh air.

Ben shifted to autopilot and grabbed the miniature fire extinguisher from underneath the kitchen sink. He removed the pin and soaked the fire. It only took a few strong blasts to put it out, leaving behind nothing but charred detritus.

The table itself didn't have so much as a single char mark marring its surface. It made no sense, but he chose to be grateful for this result instead of afraid it. The last thing he wanted to do was go out and purchase replacement furniture for the cabin.

Once he was certain the book's remains were cooled off enough to touch, he picked them up. Before Ben could take two steps, the remnants sprang out before him and turned to ash. In the blink of an eye, there was no physical evidence left to prove the book had ever existed. He started to ruminate over this but was blindsided by the sudden and overwhelming memory of having sex with Kyra.

He looked down at himself and was shocked to see his naked body. Was there any truth to his memory? It was ludicrous, but that didn't stop him from dashing back to the bedroom. As expected, the room was empty, but there was evidence of strong nocturnal emissions. Rather than chide himself this time, Ben acknowledged such things were natural.

It might even help speed up the recovery process.

Relieved by his own sense of acceptance, yet still buzzing from the unexpected adrenaline rush, Ben was lodged halfway between the urge to stay up and the pull of the sleep aid that still coursed through his body. Uncertain how to proceed and slick with terror sweat, he got dressed and slipped out of the cabin.

CHAPTER TWENTY-THREE

"Pick up the phone, goddammit!" Doug exploded.

He and Ryan had alternated phone duties for almost two weeks, but neither had gotten any useful results. It had now been three weeks since Ben left, which was one week longer than his planned trip.

Despite their constant efforts, no one from the resort had answered even a single call. The hotel's voicemail was still acting up, too, leaving Doug, Ryan, and Ben's other friends without an easy solution to their problem.

Enraged, Doug went to the resort's Facebook page for the dozenth time and posted a comment. These efforts were never replied to, but someone flagged each comment as spam and they disappeared. The same thing happened on Instagram, and his Twitter posts never went through at all.

The police department located closest to the resort was no help, either. They shrugged off Doug's concerns and intimated he was being crazy. The only good news that came from one of his many discussions with the clearly annoyed officers was the knowledge that the resort was fully operational, with no other recent issues reported. During his last call, the beleaguered sounding sheriff had consented to speak with him.

"Listen, I understand and can appreciate you think your friend is missing. But he's an adult, and vacationers often unplug from their phones and extend their stay. In fact, one of my officers checked out your friend's Facebook page a couple days ago, and there were several new posts showing him having fun in Virginia Beach."

"That's impossible! No, there haven't been any posts on his social media accounts for almost a month," Doug said.

"Maybe he blocked you from seeing them for some reason, fella, but I assure you, they're there. Virginia Beach is lovely this time of year. If you can't get a hold of him, you should come down here and check the area out for yourself. Unfortunately, there's little else I can do. I'm already swamped with legitimate cases."

"But," Doug interrupted.

"Young man, I quite simply don't have enough time or resources to devote to looking for an adult who no one else seems to think is missing. I mean, where are the calls from his family if this is true?"

Doug tried to interject that he was the closest thing Ben had to family these days, but the sheriff was on a roll and verbally bowled him over.

"Why did he post a selfie on the beach just four days ago if he's been missing for weeks? I have to get back to solving murders and looking for children who we know are missing. Can you imagine telling a parent we have to pull some of the resources allocated to their missing or murdered child's case because someone on vacation decided to turn off their phone? I'd be lynched.

"Now listen and listen good; unless you get actual proof that some type of crime has been committed, stop calling here. In fact, if you call here again without a damn good reason, I'm going to contact your local sheriff and tell 'em to pick you up for harassing an officer of the law. I'm a patient man, but my patience with this story has run out. Goodbye."

Doug's head swirled with the information that Ben supposedly had new social media posts. Had something soured between them without his realizing it? Confused, Doug reached out to Brad and Stephen again. They each confirmed what he already knew to be true; there wasn't anything new on Facebook or anywhere else. The Virginia Beach officer must have looked at the wrong account.

That figures.

"No wonder Virginia Beach is in the top third of all U.S. cities, crime-wise," he said to Ryan before filling him in about the phone call.

"I don't want to freak you out... but babe, I read something this morning about Virginia having the highest missing children rate in the country. I know Ben isn't a child, but... I don't know, I mean, maybe we *should* go look for him. The cops clearly aren't going to help us. We could go to that resort and find out what's really going on. And, if need be, we can put up missing posters all over town until something turns up," Ryan said.

Doug's eyes filled with tears, both at the crime statistic Ryan had mentioned and at his husband's offer to go with him to Virginia Beach.

A short time later, the two had booked a redeye flight and started packing.

Doug hoped this was the right thing to do. Neither of them had ever been to Virginia Beach, and he had no clue where to start, aside from the hotel. They would also have a mere three days due to the restrictions of Ryan's work schedule. Still, it was a start, and Doug was determined to do something. Any action they took would be more productive than what the cops had in mind, which apparently amounted to nothing at all.

CHAPTER TWENTY-FOUR

The crisp fall air pricked Ben's skin like thousands of tiny knives. The moisture wicked away, and his body temperature dropped below the normal range. He shivered and longed for his thin fall hoodie, but this didn't prevent his feet from wandering down the nature trail. Light from the grinning full moon bathed the ground in shimmery opulence. He could've sworn the aroma of apples and pumpkin pie lingered in the air.

He crossed over the property line in pursuit of those delicious smells, but his efforts were hindered by the sudden and inexplicable absence of moonlight. Craning his neck to glance backward, he saw nothing but an inky darkness that blotted out the entire sky. There was no moon, no stars, and no semblance of any type of light or life, yet he still plunged forward into the unknown.

Before the darkness had fallen, his nimble, surefooted movements had carried him across the landscape without disturbing the night. Without the moon's light guiding his way, his limbs now crashed gracelessly against everything, and his feet managed to find, and snap, every twig.

Breaking the serenity left him annoyed and distracted. Perhaps this state of mind made him lose track of his bearings, or maybe there was magic afoot. Either way, he soon found himself in the same scorched clearing within the woods that had spoiled his attempt at destressing with meditation.

Am I dreaming?

The night hastily fled from the daytime as if it was a child being chased by a monster. The area had been bathed in darkness mere seconds before, but now it was flooded with harsh, garish sunlight.

Some scientists say humans inherit fears from their forefathers. In this moment, Ben's brain screamed 'DANGER' as he absorbed the residual terror bequeathed to him from the banished moon. Without warning, his body changed. Bones snapped and his limbs contorted as feathers thrust forth from his skin. The biggest shock of all was that none of this hurt or shocked him in the slightest.

I guess werewolf stories are even more full of shit than I thought.

Flexing his powerful wings and taking to the sky, Ben intuitively understood he'd shapeshifted into the lead vulture. Reveling in the experience of flying with ease, it surprised him to learn he had first-hand awareness of the bird's digestion process. There was no doubt about what was being digested, either.

It was distressing at first, but when he allowed himself to give into the knowledge that his human eyeballs and intestines were marinating in his current stomach's acid juices, he felt awed by how liberating it was. Gone was the frailty of the human condition. In its place was nothing but power.

Giving into the process enabled him to take complete control of his winged actions. He also enjoyed assuming leadership over the other birds. His first act as leader was to shepherd his flock back to the tasty scraps of his human life. Together, they finished picking apart his carcass, then they pushed off into the air and soared through it with ease, canvassing several miles in mere moments. Although their recent food wasn't even digested, they kept their eyes open for their next meal.

They soon passed out of the woods and into a cityscape, flying over the majority of the town without much to capture their attention. Their luck changed when they heard the high-pitched squealing of tires that could only come from a precipitous car accident.

The vulture part of him kicked into hyperdrive, and he descended toward the noise. While flying downward, vulture Ben got a glimpse of a black car colliding with a silver car. The man in the black vehicle got out and started to walk, but the woman in the silver vehicle didn't move at all. His body twitched with excitement. The woman was dead, and he was going to clean up the mess.

Humans are so filthy, leaving so much of their waste behind and burying the rest.

He was proud to be part of a species that didn't add to the planet's environmental nightmare by being so shortsighted. Vultures understood it was better to let nothing go to waste. This accident would be no exception.

He and the other two birds arrived unnoticed on the scene. The man who'd gotten out of the black vehicle sat motionless and faceless on the side of the road. No one else was around, nor were there any noises of any kind. He landed on the ground next to the mangled silver vehicle and took a welcome whiff of the delicious mixture of blood and death.

With mounting anticipation, he reached out for the door. His vulture wings had human hands sprouting from them. This allowed him to open the car door and pull the girl's body free of the wreckage.

His cold, uncaring eyes look down at his next meal. It was Kyra. He faltered imperceptibly, then lowered his head toward her body and let the pecking begin.

The human part of his brain screamed out in pain as the vulture he'd become dined upon the rotting carcass of his fiancée, but no amount of protests could stop the beak from moving. In less time than Ben would've thought possible, he and the other birds had picked her bones clean. He took one last glance at her skeletal frame before he pushed off into the air yet again.

His body morphed back into his human form while he gained altitude. But instead of being whole, he was in the picked apart state from his ill-fated meditation session. Before he noticed this, his body parts floated freely through the air. But as soon as Ben became aware of the change, he lost the ability to fly.

There was no pain at all when his body crashed into the earth, causing his vestigial remains to became liquefied. A small fire sprang up, but it was soon extinguished in an insignificant puff of smoke. After the smoke dissipated, he somehow saw the ground. It showed only one small char mark as evidence of his passing.

CHAPTER TWENTY-FIVE

Three Months Ago

Kyra's wake was set to start at four o'clock in the afternoon. At four-fifteen, the Hindu ceremonial recitation of mantras still hadn't started. Even through his overwhelming grief, Ben bristled at what he perceived as a slight against his fiancée's memory. She had always been early for everything. The idea of people gathering to say goodbye to her without properly observing the time twisted his stomach.

I'm so sorry, Kyra.

His shoulders, covered in the fine black suit jacket he had purchased for their wedding, hitched as the latest sob caught in his throat. The more he tried to maintain his composure, the larger the sob became; it had started life as little more than a small pebble but had since reached the size of a softball.

Unable to hold on any longer, grief streamed down his face for the first time since entering the funeral home. Hot, salty liquid seeped into some fresh cuts on his face and neck, making him wince. At the same time, the sob broke free of his throat with as much power and force as a rock hurled by a slingshot into a glass bottle.

A few people glanced in his direction, but no one made eye contact. Ben realized he was the only person crying. He understood this was part of the reverential Hindu way of saying goodbye to their loved ones, but it still brought goosebumps to his flesh.

How can they look so calm?

A warm, firm hand landed on his shoulder before the tears stopped. Sniffling and wiping his face, Ben turned his head to the left to see exactly who he knew would be by his side.

"Hi Doug," he choked out.

His best friend nodded at him, then wrapped him in a bearhug. "You don't have to do any of this alone. I'm here. We're here," Doug said in a voice just loud enough for Ben to comprehend.

At eighteen minutes past four, Kyra's family called for everyone to gather together. Her brother, Neerav, defied the silent nature of his given name by saying a few words. Only tiny snippets made it past the rushing, roaring train that seemed to have taken up residence inside of Ben's ears. However, what he did hear, and what he could discern from the mixed snippets of English and Hindi, weaved together a fitting eulogy for his lost love.

As the service shifted into the next phase, Neerav and several others chanted rhythmically. Ben was clueless about their first mantra's meaning, but he inferred from everyone's actions that it was some type of prayer.

The mantras continued for quite some time, during which each person chanting looked inside the simple, non-adorned white box that held Kyra's body. Once they were all done, it was Ben's turn to say goodbye.

His body resisted, and he had to struggle to prevent himself from breaking into a run in the opposite direction. With a gentle, barely perceptible push from Doug, his feet moved toward the casket. Looking down at her caused a slight gasp to escape Ben's lips.

You look so far away.

Fresh tears welled up in his eyes. Hindu tradition dictated looking at this as a celebration instead of a cause for a sadness, but he couldn't help it. He also wasn't Hindu, so he figured it was permissible to show at least a smidge of his true feelings.

Kyra was an organ donor, and he was certain her organs had been harvested at the hospital after she was pronounced dead. It was a bit shocking to see someone could have their organs removed without looking any skinnier. He had been nervous about seeing her deflated and was relieved his fears were unfounded.

He reached into the coffin and took her hand. An audible gasp emanated from a few onlookers, along with the buzz of several voices condemning this action. The Hindu funeral ceremony dictates that no one should touch the body after it has been cleaned and prepared, especially a non-Hindu. His impulsive act violated this ritualized behavior, making the body impure before the final step: cremation. Self-consciously, he removed his hand much faster than he would have preferred.

A short time later, Kyra's mother, Shivani, approached Ben. Unlike most of Kyra's family, she didn't hesitate to look in his eyes. She also didn't make any attempt to hide the hardness within hers, nor did she hide her revulsion at the bruises and cuts on his face. She might have celebrated her daughter's passing publicly in the way her religion dictated, but she was clearly angry about it.

"Ben, Kyra was happiest with you. I'm not okay or forgiving about the loss of my daughter, but I don't want to punish those who were closest to her, either." There might have been truth in her words, but the cold tone in Shivani's voice made them seem like nothing more than forced social niceties. "Nature, the environment... those are... were the other loves of her life. She had a funeral plan, Ben. Did you know that?"

His eyes opened wide in shock. Not trusting himself to speak, he shook his head.

"She always was ahead of everyone else, no?"

This time, Ben nodded yes. It made perfect sense, but it was stunning nonetheless that someone so young, and with so much vitality, had already planned her own funeral.

"Her ashes are to be buried beneath the sapling of an oak tree so she can 'be one with nature' throughout eternity. This isn't entirely in keeping with the Hindu faith, but you know how strong-willed she could be."

Shivani's face hardened, and the thin wrinkles on her medium-olive skin became much more apparent. "You also know she was walking away from that path. Something we suspect *you* had a hand in."

Seething, Shivani appeared to almost have smoke coming from her ears. Seeing this from across the room, Neerav came to the rescue. He was more religious than Kyra, but he also had a modern view of the world.

"Mother, let's not impugn Kyra's motives. Have you asked him yet?"

She shook her head, opened her mouth, shut it again, then made a frustrated sound. "You do it!" she said while stalking away.

Embarrassed, Neerav's dark skin deepened further as his cheeks flushed. "I'm sorry about that, Ben. But you have to understand... we have a lot of unanswered questions, and where there are questions, there's anger. For example, what the hell was she doing out so late?"

Without pausing so much as a beat to wait for a response, he said, "You know what? Never mind. What's done is done. Ben... my sister wanted you to bury her urn and plant the oak tree sapling. Can you do this for us? For her?"

An imaginary vacuum removed every thought from his brain and siphoned the saliva from his mouth. He stared at Neerav in confusion for so long it became uncomfortable for both men. Just before Kyra's brother gave up on him, a hollow "Yes" managed to escape.

"Thank you. I'll come by your place tomorrow with the urn and the tree. Does eleven a.m. work for you?"

Not waiting for a reply, Neerav turned to walk away, but hesitated. Looking back over his slender shoulder, he raised an eyebrow toward Ben's black eye while issuing a parting shot, "Don't let me find out my sister died because of something illegal."

Stunned by this insinuation, Ben returned to Doug's side. He also noticed for the first time that Stephen, Mark, and Ryan had all shown up. With one last, longing look toward everything he'd lost, he allowed his friends to remove him from the funeral home so the family could move on to the cremation phase in private. Every other attendee who wasn't an immediate family member shuffled out together.

Ben's shock-induced state made it easier to let his friends call the shots for the next couple of hours. He soon found himself sitting on a couch at Doug and Ryan's place, with a beer to his left and a plate of uneaten food in his lap. The only things he was fully conscious of were the task Neerav had given him and the continual, one-sided, internal discussion he kept having with the deceased love of his life.

I shouldn't be the one to do this for you, Kyra. I shouldn't have even agreed. But he said this is what you wanted, and there's no way I'm going to deny you your last wish. If only I could somehow make it so that your last wish didn't need to be told today, or anytime during the next several decades. It's not fair. You should be alive and well, Kyra. I'd give anything to be able to trade places with you. I miss you so much.

CHAPTER TWENTY-SIX

Present Day

Ben's feet were torn apart from a night spent wandering in the woods. He had no idea how he'd gotten outside or why he'd spent the night there, but he had the oddest inkling he'd eaten something strange. There were also a few lingering whispers in his mind about flying, but he dismissed them without giving it a second thought.

He made his way back down the wooded trail in time to see the sun rise over the water. With his back to the cabin, he sat in awe of what his mother had once called 'nature's morning miracle.' Even as a kid, he'd thought the phrase was corny, but he now yearned to hear it again.

As the allure of sunrise passed, he turned toward the back door and was startled by the unexpected sight of decaying ivy covering the entire exterior of the cabin. It had even strangled the back door in an interminable mess. Intimidated, Ben attempted to fight his way through the thicket and into the cabin, but he couldn't find the door handle.

Rushing to the front of the building, he knew what he would find before getting there; that door had been eaten by ivy, too. Unsure what to do, his eyes darted around the lawn until they fell upon a hatchet.

Grinning with preordained success, he leapt at the hatchet and hacked maniacally at the oppressive vines. He'd expected a big struggle that would paint him as a valiant hero overcoming unimaginable odds, but the mess of ivy shrank away with each chop. Cutting through it was on par with separating warm butter from its container.

The physical task wasn't what left him reeling. Walking inside the cabin and turning around to shut the door was much worse; all the vines he'd cleared away were choking the open exit. Only now they were much thicker and nastier, with huge thorns that threatened to rip him apart. With an anguished howl, he remembered tossing the hatchet to the ground before coming inside.

How am I ever going to get out again?

* * * * *

What happened last night? Think, damn it.

Ben was distressed by the unpleasantness of déjà vu. Here he was, sitting on the couch at Cabin Green, flooded with the oddest, most disorienting half-formed memories. Even worse, he had no idea how he'd been transported from flying through the air as a vulture to sitting here like everything was normal. Well, everything aside from the ivy crushing the cabin, anyway.

Maybe he hadn't gone outside at all and it was just an acutely weird dream? His feet corroborated his fading memories, though. They were scratched up and swollen, which seemed indicative of a night spent wandering the woods barefoot. With each passing second, the details of what he thought he remembered were rendered obsolete.

Am I losing my mind?

The constant uncertainty caused Ben to doubt everything he thought he knew, both about the last few weeks and his entire life in general. It had even started picking at his belief system. As a result, he wondered for the first time in years if there was even the slightest possibility God did exist... or at least the Devil.

He wasn't sure he wanted to live in a world presided over by a God who would've taken Kyra from him in such a horrible way. It hadn't been fair to anyone and had left an indelible mark of sadness on all who'd known her. How could a God allow something like that to happen to one of its most beautiful creations? It didn't make any sense, and Ben's mind rallied against it, as always. This time his convictions were on shakier ground than usual, but he still refused to admit that out loud.

There wasn't much he could think of to do as a distraction, so he reached for a smoke. As he lit up, Ben realized he only had five cigarettes left.

"Dammit!"

The easy solution would be going into town to get new cigarettes, do a load of laundry, and pick up some provisions. This was thwarted by a serious complication. He'd already tried both doors and all the windows and had found that escape was no longer just elusive; it was flat out impossible unless an axe or a flamethrower materialized out of thin air. In other words, the easy solution wasn't going to be an option.

Ben's concern skyrocketed as he did a mental tally of what was left and how long it would last. He could make it maybe two more days with the smokes and four more days with the food. Tomorrow would be his last time wearing clean clothing.

If I ration the supplies, I could probably stretch them another day or two. And I can hand wash some clothes.

This wasn't palatable, but he would do what was necessary. Leaving just didn't seem like an option, and he wasn't sure if it would become one in four or five days, either. He was beginning to believe he would pass the rest of his existence in the little cabin. Part of him didn't care at all if this was true, but the thought also caused a sinking sensation in the pit of his stomach.

Ben wanted to make something to eat, but rationing meant holding off hunger for as long as possible. Letting his mind linger unoccupied by distractions would make things much worse. Faced with two viable options, showering or playing cards, he opted for the former.

Determined to do the nicest thing possible for himself, he cranked the hot water up so high the bathroom soon appeared to be cloaked in fog. Scrubbing his skin clean brought him pleasure, which was in far too short of supply these days.

Standing under the shower head with his eyes closed, Ben once again heard the protests of whatever lurked in the water pipes. The noises still concerned him, but they'd taken a back seat to his need for normality. Allowing the warm liquid to run over his body opened his mind and purged the day's most distressing memories. Soon, he felt at ease in his surroundings and his confidence grew.

I don't know why I was hellbent on leaving. This is so nice and relaxing. I'll make a nice meal after, then maybe go for a boat ride.

Pleased with his plans but in no hurry to leave the shower, he ignored the water's sudden staccato effect. Harsh, almost clumpy water hit his chest and head, but with his newfound mellow vibe, Ben couldn't be bothered to lift his eyelids. A drastic change in water temperature did the trick, though, and his eyes flew open while he jumped backward.

Blurriness greeted him as the water attacked his skin with hard, frigid bursts. The inconsistent stream clued him into the fact that something wasn't right. His hand moved lazily toward the knobs to turn up the heat when the signals transmitting from his eyes into his brain managed to elicit a more appropriate response.

Ben's scream echoed off the shower's glass door. He'd been bathing in something that wasn't water at all. The discolored mixture contained greenish-yellow bile tinted with what could only be blood.

He ran from the shower so fast that he slipped and came dangerously close to bashing his head. After surviving unscathed, he rubbed his body with a dirty towel, but the stubborn stains remained etched on his skin. Pleading with the world to give him a break, he attempted to get out the backdoor.

I won't even go anywhere, just please, please, let me jump into the lake.

The door refused to budge, and hysteria bubbled up out of his mouth as shrieks announced his disdain. Determined not to live another minute covered in what he assumed was someone else's vomit and blood, he marched into the kitchen and had a face-off with the sink.

Are you going to betray me, too? Should I risk it?

Out of choices, Ben nudged the faucet on before running five paces away. He glanced wearily at it, fearful something even worse might come out such as a venomous snake or thousands of fire ants. Much to his relief, none of these horrible daymares came true. Clean water gushed from the tap. Still suspicious, he ignored the hot water altogether and let the cold water run for several minutes before trusting it enough to wash the filth from his skin.

That was the last shower I'll ever take here.

CHAPTER TWENTY-SEVEN

His food supplies were almost gone, but there were still enough coffee beans left to provide a mind-clearing caffeine jolt. The enticing aroma permeated his nasal cavities as he enjoyed one of the finest cups of coffee he'd ever ingested. He savored the rich, full-bodied flavor, along with the fresh, heady smell. At that moment, Ben decided maybe life did have enough small pleasures to make it worth living.

His stomach wasn't full after every single drop of coffee was gone, but the hunger pangs and cravings had subsided, at least for the moment. Taking advantage of this, he shuffled the worn deck of cards and laid out another game of solitaire. Ben pondered over the implications of the inventor's life. Were they as lonely then as he was now? Or did solitude open the doors of creativity?

Maybe I should invent a new card game.

With nothing better to do, he proceeded to pass the next several hours playing a variety of card games. Some of them required severe alterations so they could be played alone, but he didn't mind changing things up a bit.

For some inexplicable reason, he now believed the deck of cards would help guide him away from this madness. There was an unknown question buzzing around the cabin, and the cards whispered that they knew the answer. If he played them correctly, everything would be revealed. He knew this sounded crazy and was also pretty sure it was nothing more than a combination of superstition and cabin fever talking. Still, there was no harm in going ahead and playing a bunch of card games anyway, right?

When he could stand it no longer, Ben walked into the kitchen to get something to eat. Rather than make the sandwich his cravings longed for, he toasted two pieces of bread and ate them with only a glass of water for accompaniment. It wasn't satisfying, but it did take the edge off his hunger.

With the meager food attempting to fill his empty stomach, he was met by the typical, Pavlovian urge for nicotine. This would be the hardest thing of all to ration, but also perhaps the most critical.

He'd tried to quit smoking in the past, and it hadn't been pretty. When talking to others about this failed attempt, Ben likened the ordeal to having been trapped inside of a self-imposed prison modeled on the penal system in third world countries. He knew this was melodramatic, but to the other people in his life who had tried to deal with his nicotine withdrawal, it probably seemed rather accurate.

He sat down at the kitchen table and began to devise a plan for how best to utilize his last five cigarettes. Ben was all too aware that if he didn't have at least a bit of nicotine in his system at most times, he would suffer terribly. History told him that he was 'lucky' enough to have every single side effect of nicotine withdrawal, including the rare ones.

But when I get out of here, I'm going to quit for good.

He soon settled on a plan intended to stretch each cigarette over an entire day. Instead of savoring the experience, he would light them long enough to get two to three hits, but that was it. Ben put this into practice immediately by allowing himself to have the first two hits of the day. They were good, but just like his meal, they were not satisfying.

His quick burst of nicotine was followed by a return to the card games. He would have preferred to take a walk, but there was only so much pacing he could do within the limited confines of the cabin.

Tired of solitaire, Ben played the card game War. This required a minimum of two players, so he battled against himself. Not exactly an exciting way to pass the time, but it did amuse him to keep track of which part of himself won each game. For humorous purposes, he'd split himself into part A and part B, then made internal bets over which part would succeed.

At some level, he understood that purposefully giving himself two personalities, even if just for a card game, was not a very mentally sound thing to do, but he did it anyway. To rule out any inner squabbling caused by competitiveness, he played himself to a draw.

Bored with games and with nowhere to go, he opted to lie down for a while. Instead of drifting back to sleep, he enjoyed the sunlight streaming over his body and was soon surprised to find himself aroused. He lowered his hand to the front of his boxer shorts and pulled himself free of the cotton material. He had nothing and no one specific in mind, but he hadn't ever needed that to bring himself to an orgasm.

For the first time in more than thirteen weeks, he allowed his mind to wander down its inner hallways while indulging in the most basic of human pleasures. After the first few minutes, Ben didn't think about anything. There was no cabin in the woods, there was no dead fiancée, and there was certainly no supernatural activity.

As his climax grew near, Ben had the inexplicable thought that he was being watched. This caused him to hesitate, and the loss of momentum pushed his orgasm away. Annoyed, he started up again while forcing the paranoid thoughts from his mind.

He worked himself back up to the precipice of an orgasm and was almost there when the sensation of being watched stole over him once again. He paused and looked over both his shoulders but saw nothing there. With an angry, self-directed grunt, Ben ordered himself to not let a non-existent distraction get in the way again.

Although paranoia initially returned in mass quantities, he soon slipped into a fantasy of making love to Kyra in a white room filled with white flowers, accompanied by a white silken bed sheet on top of a new bed. The moment was beautiful, but just like a dream, it didn't last.

His eyes opened and the stingy haze of dripping sweat obscured his vision. When clear sight finally returned, he realized he was the only one moving. Kyra was still there, but she seemed detached from the situation. Her eyes had become cold and unfocused, and they stared past him to the ceiling.

In his confusion, he almost didn't perceive the other subtle changes that had occurred in the room. The bright whiteness had transformed into nothing but a dank darkness. While thrusting yet again, his foot slipped and connected with something that didn't feel like part of the bed. Ben's eyes glanced to the right and reported something his brain refused to believe.

That's impossible.

He appealed his case by looking to the right again, followed by the left, but this didn't change the evidence at hand. As he neared his climax, he looked more closely at Kyra and realized the truth of what he was doing. Her dearth of movement and complete lack of feedback was explained by the fact that he was assaulting her dead body. Even worse, the bed he'd first envisioned had transformed into the coffin she was cremated in. He heard the shocked and dismayed gasps of every person who had attended her wake.

Oh my god.

Panic took over his mind, but his body still delivered a much-delayed orgasm. As waves of pleasure flooded forth, Ben was floored with the realization of what he'd done and how sick it was.

I just fantasized about fucking my dead fiancée's body in front of her family and friends, and in a coffin, no less. What the fuck is wrong with me?

Forgetting about the mystery of whether or not someone was watching him, Ben ran into the bathroom and promptly threw up his last meal.

CHAPTER TWENTY-EIGHT

Ben's remorse plagued his mind and body for a short while before it evaporated. The queasiness abated completely, replaced by the peaceful sleepiness of his recent orgasm. Along with this newfound sense of ease went the last vestiges of feeling watched or of being disturbed by his now forgotten dark fantasy. With a slight smile on his face, he gave into the second urge of the morning and went back to sleep.

His dreams weren't nearly as deep or terrifying this time around; instead, they all revolved around sex. He had dreams of being with Kyra, followed by several other nighttime fantasies, ranging from hooking up with faceless women to copulating with what he believed to be a werewolf.

It didn't surprise him to wake up and find that he'd soiled the sheets, but it did bother him that he had no real method for getting them cleaned. Regardless of everything else happening around him, he still desired cleanliness almost as much as a solid meal.

He'd been able to hand wash some of his smaller items in the kitchen sink, which had so far prevented him from deteriorating into a stinking, dirty mess. The enormous task of somehow getting his sheets clean was more than he could handle, though. Yanking them from the bed, he concluded he'd have to sleep directly on the mattress now.

Yet another basic comfort you've taken from me. Bastard.

Embittered and needing solace more than anything else, he permitted himself to have one slice of toast and finished the last three hits of his current cigarette. There were now only four left, and it took an enormous amount of willpower to push aside the anxiety that rose up within his stomach and chest every time he looked inside the nearly empty box.

Rationally, Ben knew he should be much more concerned about the food running out, but that didn't make his chest constrict nearly as much as the sight of only four more cigarettes. He was not ready to deal with nicotine withdrawal again, especially not the type that wasn't even self-inflicted.

Wait, why can't I just leave?

Ben's elusive memories had slipped again. He looked with longing toward the clear windows. They didn't display even a hint of ivy.

I thought...

Without giving it much thought, he broke through what seemed to be little more than an unspoken taboo by moving toward the front door.

I don't know why I'm so afraid of this.

His thoughts tried to push him forward like a brave knight, but his muscle memory needed a lot more cajoling. Wincing as if he expected it to scorch him, he tapped out at the knob with his right pointer finger. Nothing happened.

Relaxing slightly, he gripped the knob with his right hand and attempted to twist it. Again, nothing happened.

Fear swelled up in his stomach. The door wouldn't budge; he was really stuck here. While attempting once more to open it, a memory floated through his mind; he'd done almost this exact same thing a few days ago.

He didn't know if the memory was true, but it had a distinctly authentic feel. If that was the case, he was apparently running in circles, forgetting what he'd done and tried from day-to-day. Confusion and fear overwhelmed his senses. Was he somehow misplacing individual memories? What about entire days?

When something happened like this, his mind always jumped to the worst-case scenario. This time, he became convinced he was developing signs of a serious mental illness. His mother wasn't the only one in the family to have issues with mental health, and he was very concerned about ending up stuck on meds or, even worse, committed for life.

In his panic, Ben shoved his shoulder against the door and jiggled the knob up and down. The door gave no signs of giving into his demands, but his continued efforts turned more frantic by the second. With a horrifying clunk, the doorknob broke off in his hand, leaving the door even more firmly attached to its frame. It was official; there would be no getting out of the front door.

He paced back and forth through the tiny kitchen and commanded himself to calm down. This didn't help, so he ran into the dining room and clawed at the window, only to discover that the lock latch had rusted into the locked position. No matter how much Ben banged against it, the rusty latch refused to budge.

Without thinking through the consequences, he picked up one of the wooden kitchen table chairs and threw it at the glass. The glass didn't even ripple under the impact, but the chair was thrown back with immense force and landed in shards.

Sweat ran down his face and soaked the back of his shirt. There was nothing silly or superstitious about it. He was truly stuck with minimal provisions and nothing aside from a deck of cards and an almost dead iPhone to keep his mind from eroding. In that moment, Ben decided the single scariest thing he could think of was being locked inside of a tiny cabin with no supplies and a potential ghost problem.

It was no longer taking much of a leap of faith for him to believe there were many more ghosts inside of this cabin than just Kyra, who had resided within his mind for months. The cabin ghosts seemed to have malevolent intentions, and he was almost positive it was their goal to drive him insane. That or kill him, whichever came first.

Ben looked around the cabin for anything that would help keep him rooted in reality. What he saw made things much worse, rather than better. The mantel above the fireplace had somehow been ransacked, and the puzzle box no longer sat where it normally resided.

A shudder of fear coursed throughout his body, and he forced himself to turn and face the dining room table. The puzzle was there, fully intact and ready to taunt him. He was one-hundred percent certain that it had not been there when he'd thrown a chair at the window. How could it have gotten off the mantel and become assembled without his noticing?

He couldn't imagine a ghost having that kind of power. Even more terrifying was the thought of what he would see in the puzzle. The notion of looking was unbearable, but he also couldn't tear his eyes away.

Against his will, Ben walked closer to the table and lowered his head to see what impossible insidiousness was coming next. He stumbled backward in shock upon discovering the puzzle no longer contained a picture of the Golden Gate Bridge. It now depicted a desolate stretch of road with two cars in the distance, heading from different directions toward the same general area.

As soon as his eyes fell upon the scene, it turned into a moving picture. The cars went into motion, the wind whipped through the trees, and a noticeable hum sang from both engines. Ben knew what the scene was depicting, and he wanted nothing to do with it. In fear and disgust, he closed his eyes and turned away from the disturbing image. It played on regardless, and the sounds that emanated from the puzzle continued to fill up the space around him.

"Please don't do this to me," he begged of the air. "I can't endure this." His voice trailed off, and the tears he'd been keeping at bay rose to the surface again.

"Oh, but you will endure it," a monstrous voice said.

He literally jumped an inch at the sound of someone else's voice. Before he even hit the ground he was in motion, running at full speed into the back porch. He smacked against the back door with a thud; it refused to budge. He pushed, clawed, kicked, and pleaded with the rear exit, but it remained just as steadfast as the front door.

"There's no escape," a hissing voice whispered as the speaker's breath tickled Ben's ear. He whipped his head around to face his tormenter, but there was no one there.

"What the fuck?"

He spun the rest of the way around and stumbled back into the living room. Ben steeled himself against the puzzle, resolved to avoid it at all costs. He felt violated by the knowledge that the ghost had been toying with him, but this was one game he refused to participate in.

With that in mind, he went into the bedroom and sat down on the bed. His body trembled beneath the weight of the cabin's latest revelations, and he wondered how long he could expect to survive in a place that was so obviously determined to destroy him. He also once again questioned his own mental health. Was it possible for the puzzle to have done any of the things he believed he'd seen? And what about the disembodied voice?

All the doubts, superstitions, and internal debates were forced to surface. Something wasn't right in the cabin, and he couldn't avoid the truth any longer. He believed his own mental stability, although possibly quite weak, wasn't the main culprit behind his recent experiences.

Ben chose to take a leap of faith. There was something haunting this cabin, and whatever it was, it wasn't friendly. Therefore, he needed to figure out what to do to deal with this crisis. There wasn't much that came to mind, but this was due to a lack of relevant information.

How many people have any viable ideas about how to deal with a malevolent spirit, anyway?

There was only one thing he was certain of; the ghost was not going to let him leave unless it was on its terms. To get there might require a lot of sacrifice and would almost certainly necessitate facing up to things he'd rather push away. With that being the case, he understood the necessity of going back into the dining room to look at the puzzle. He'd never wanted to do anything else less in his life, but he was convinced it was the most important first step he could take toward getting his life back.

He hesitated a while longer, then opened the bedroom door. A mind-numbingly cold blast of air greeted him. Winter had somehow settled inside the cabin while he was thinking things through. This made no sense at all because the porch had been nice and warm a couple of hours ago. Now, he could see his breath swirling around his body.

How could the temperature have dropped by approximately forty degrees in the span of less than one hour? As disturbing as the phenomenon was, it did serve as further evidence that the problems he'd been encountering were not of his own fractured mental design.

Ben crept across the floor until he stood less than two feet from the kitchen table. He stopped, pinched his eyes closed, and attempted to brace himself before stepping forward for a closer look. After a brief pause, he opened his eyes and forcibly looked down at the puzzle.

CHAPTER TWENTY-NINE

The car scene was gone, as was any other picture the puzzle had ever depicted. It was now blacker than midnight and no longer appeared to be a puzzle at all. Instead, it looked like a moving, breathing black shape. Something deep inside of it called to him, and he gave into the urge to push his head closer. Half expecting to clunk his head on the table, he was relieved and terrified when his head entered the blackness.

He could see nothing and quickly started to have second thoughts. With a jerking motion, Ben tried to whip his head out of the puzzle, but he met a force of colossal resistance. The momentary relief of a minute before curdled, and something sour flooded his mouth.

In the outside world, his hands dug into the table and tried to gain some leverage with which to pull his head free. He tugged and tugged, but it was like he was bound in place by taut invisible chains. He cried out into the darkness, but the sound was swallowed whole before reaching his ears.

Ben couldn't see it, but he experienced the sensation of his body parts being ripped apart and floating into the abyss. His anchor gone, he had no frame of reference for his current location, and his awareness of the puzzle faded into the darkness. The only certitude he could claim was that he had been broken down into the nothingness the vultures left behind.

Did I ever get away from them? Was everything else just thoughts inside a disembodied head being digested within three vultures?

In any other situation, Ben would've thought the unwelcome darkness was a byproduct of being trapped in his own mind. He had to admit that explanation seemed a lot less likely now that there was no physical brain or head left.

Perhaps he'd been ripped down to his soul? This thought plagued and reassured him, for he'd been reasonably certain for years there was no such thing as a soul. But if he'd been wrong about that, could he have been wrong about Heaven and Hell as well? Was he in Hell? Or was this some type of hallucination or dream? And if so, why couldn't he snap out of it?

Ben had nothing left to feel sensations with, yet somehow, a pervading sense of coldness washed over him. He laughed at himself, then laughed again for believing he'd actually been able to laugh. How could someone laugh without a body? The entire thing left him bewildered and exasperated. He had no eyes, yet he could see the all-encompassing darkness as vividly as anything he'd ever looked upon. He had no concrete form, yet he could sense where his limbs had been and where they should be.

Ben's mind twisted and tumbled in the space between himself and nothingness. He became convinced he was suffering from a vibrant delusion, perhaps brought on by drugs or alcohol. There could be no other explanation, and he grew increasingly certain this wasn't just some messed up dream he was going to wake up from at any moment.

As soon as that possibility had first come to him, Ben knew it was a lie. This wasn't some simple dream, nor was he drunk. He was in another place now, perhaps being punished for the sins of his waking days.

One thought kept echoing through his mind. *It's all my fault, it's all my fault.* No other thought was strong enough to overcome it or to wrest it from his consciousness.

Time passed by untold. It could've been seconds or eons, but he would never know without something else to measure its passage against. He thought he could deal with not having a solid form, but the darkness was more than he could bear.

Ben wondered what he would do if he was truly doomed to spend the rest of his life in this state, and it sent shock waves of panic throughout his phantom body. No one could survive a life lived in darkness with no chance for any other sensory input. He would never feel, hear, or smell anything ever again, with the exception of his missing body's phantom lingering pains.

Several more hours, or maybe years, passed. His brain screamed in a silent, but horrifyingly loud, outburst. If he'd possessed hands, he would've jammed them over the ears that were also missing. His anxiety mounted, and he tried without success to calm himself down.

He was bitterly amused by his constant reliance on phrases that no longer made sense. His mind kept using these worthless words in a failed attempt to catalog his current situation, and it was especially fond of the idea that he was losing his mind.

How can you lose your mind when you have no mind?

Ben decided that the stress of losing Kyra had unleashed a torrential psychotic break. He'd read about people's minds eroding in the blink of an eye, and he did have his mother's genetics.

Maybe I finally snapped. If so, where was he? What did he need to do to resurface in the land of the living?

He desperately wanted a functional body again. No ideas about how to make this come to fruition occurred to him, and time stretched out further into the infinite blackness.

CHAPTER THIRTY

One Year Ago

"Be sure to put on your fanciest clothes tomorrow, lady. I'm taking you to a nice restaurant for our anniversary!" Ben said.

"That sounds lovely!" Kyra beamed.

Twenty-four hours later, Ben looked at his reflection in the bathroom mirror. Wearing his best black suit with a white button-up shirt and a red silk tie left him uncomfortable, but he thought the temporary loss of comfort would be worth it.

Upon arriving at the restaurant, Ben noted that Kyra was five minutes ahead of him, as usual. Her predictability in this regard gave him the opportunity to show up early, but he never did. His custom had always been to arrive right on time, plus his instincts told him she enjoyed being earlier than everyone else.

Why would I ever take something away from her that brings her pleasure?

This was the first time Ben had seen Kyra dressed up, and the year-long wait was more than worthwhile. He gaped at her as she walked up to him in red strapless dress. Seeing his reaction, she stifled a self-conscious laugh before embracing him, followed by a quick kiss.

"Wow, Kyra. You look stunning!"

"Don't act so surprised, silly."

"You surprise me daily, my love. With one exception, of course."

"Five minutes early is the new on time." They both laughed while approaching the front door, arm-in-arm.

A middle-aged man with laugh lines etched into his face tipped his top hat toward them as he grabbed the ornate, heavy door handle and pulled it outward. "Enjoy your meal," he said with an air of professionalism.

They thanked him, then Kyra took in the opulence of the restaurant. "Ben... this is almost overwhelming! I mean, the fanciest place we've eaten during the past year was the Cheesecake Factory. Granted, that's actually pretty nice, but we went in wearing shorts and t-shirts."

He beamed with pride. "You deserve this, Kyra. We deserve this. I've never been happier in my entire life."

Choked up by his display of emotion, she smiled and nodded in response. The hostess led them to their reserved table. This time, they both floated to their seats.

Ben knew Kyra would be on to him due to the date and location, so he tried his best to throw her off. Long after their dishes had been cleared and they'd enjoyed a quality meal that was, in his opinion, almost worth the price, he asked her to follow him upstairs.

There were numerous gourmet restaurants throughout the Ann Arbor and Metro Detroit area, but he'd made his selection based on one vital detail: rooftop access. The Detroit skyline greeted them, as did a slightly too crisp autumn breeze. He gently took her hand and led her to a prearranged spot. There, underneath the sparkling light of dozens of visible stars, he slipped his suit jacket around her shoulders. Soft music played in the background. Although he wasn't confident in his dancing abilities, he pulled her close and they swayed from side-to-side.

"I love you, Ben."

"You are so loved, Kyra."

As the song ended, he backed one step away before lowering himself to one knee. "I've never known anyone as lovely as you. Thank you for your love and support. If you'll let me, I'll spend the rest of my life loving and supporting you in return." He paused, looked into her sparkling eyes, and said, "Will you marry me, Kyra?"

She knelt down to his level, wrapped her arms around his slender frame, and said the sweetest word in the English language: "Yes!" They embraced tightly, almost as if their lives depended on it. It was the happiest, brightest moment of his life.

Afterwards, they went to his apartment and made love for hours. It had always been special with her, but this time was beyond anything he had ever experienced. In the afterglow, she looked at him with a sense of wonderment and contentment. He missed that look and her brilliant smile most of all.

CHAPTER THIRTY-ONE

Present Day

Ben was in the darkest state of his life. Kyra's death had been enough to shatter his world, and now a series of increasingly disturbing and potentially deadly encounters left him doubting his mental stability. The icing on this Gothically black cake was being stuck in absolute darkness with no idea how, or if, he could return to normal life.

He wondered if sleep and dreams existed in this void. Such an escape would be more welcome now than it had ever been at any other point during his life. In dreams, he might be able to see something again as opposed to floating in nothing. He no longer cared what that something would be, as he reasoned that anything had to be better than darkness. Mankind's intrinsic fear of the dark had never made more sense or hit closer to home than it did right now.

He spoke, but there was no actual sound within the vacuum of blackness that he was residing in. "Please. What's happening to me?"

A few more moments of contemplation passed, then a colossal wave of depression washed over him. "My fault, my fault, my fault."

Ben's mind was ravaged, leaving him feeling worthless. The blackness overwhelming his thoughts had become even more complete and less forgiving than the physical darkness that surrounded him.

It was like being in a prison cell within purgatory, two life sentences left to be meted out over the course of eternity. Within the depression, he found a form of acceptance. This was what his life was now, and it was better than what he deserved. He had spent the past three months living a hollowed-out existence anyway, at least here he could receive the punishment that he had long felt he deserved.

"My fault, my fault, my fault..."

As the burden of knowledge set in, long repressed memories resurfaced. They were all horrible beyond belief and left him emotionally cut into tiny, inconsequential pieces.

How could his life have led him to this moment? It wasn't meant to be like this. Kyra was supposed to be his bride. They were going to have their version of happily ever after, but now her ashes were either rotting in the ground or her body had been eaten by a vulture containing his mind. He was left faceless and voiceless in a void of nothing but his own self-loathing. What a perfect ending to his perfectly plotted out life.

He knew his only chance at survival was to finally face up to his demons. It was well past time to take on his fears and the darkness.

His hands once again found purchase on the sides of the table. At first, his fresh struggles were met by a strong pressure on his neck and back. As he continued to fight against his unseen oppressor, he finally gained the upper hand.

Flying backward, his head came out of the puzzle. At the same time, his body soared in reverse until he slammed against the wall next to the enclosed porch. The speed with which he hit the wall jarred his entire body, made a couple of teeth come loose, and caused him to black out.

Many hours passed before his eyelids attempted to open. Once they accomplished this task, he had to rub them several times to wipe away the blurriness in his vision.

The first thing Ben observed after normal vision returned was that the deep freeze in the cabin had ended. In its place was a fire roaring inside of the fireplace. On the plus side, it was well-made and contained, so he supposed he had worse things to worry about than a fire that had miraculously sprung to life. It might have even kept him from freezing to death.

He stood on shaking legs and walked over to the kitchen table. The puzzle was no longer there. A glance at the mantel showed Ben it was back in its typical resting place. He no longer cared how it had gotten put away; he was simply relieved it wasn't out to mock him anymore. He had a strong desire to throw the wretched thing into the fire, but instinctually understood the ghost – *or whatever it is* - would never allow that. It would probably only rile the dark entity up again, so he forced away the satisfying mental image of the puzzle being burned into embers.

At a loss for any concrete direction to take, he went about his newly tweaked daily routine. First, he ate a meager amount of food, followed by taking three hits off a cigarette. Next, he contemplated taking a shower, but something about it brought a crawling creepiness over his entire body, so he chose to skip it for the day.

Ben paced throughout the cabin. He needed to find something other than card games to occupy his mind, but his options were markedly limited. His phone came to mind for the first time in days. Now seemed like the perfect time to see if any of his friends had replied to his numerous messages. As he scrolled through his texts, Ben's eyes began to well up. There were replies, all right, and they were all horrible.

Stephen: *"Wow, man. Wow. You've clearly lost it. Stop texting and calling me. I'm done."*

Mark: *"Was that supposed to be funny or something? What the fuck is wrong with you? Even I wouldn't attempt to make a joke out of something like that. You're sick in the head, man. It's time to get help."*

Worst of all was the text message from his best friend.

Doug: *"You SLEPT with Ryan? Why the FUCK would you text me such an insane thing? If you're lying, you're a fucking douchebag. If you're not lying, you're the worst person on the planet. Either way, I don't ever want to speak to you again. Get fucked, Ben. Friendship over."*

Stunned, he sat the phone down. Everyone who mattered to him was gone. He didn't know what the hell any of them were talking about, of course. He hadn't texted them anything vile, and he certainly never claimed to have slept with Doug's husband.

"It has to be the cabin. Cabin Green is destroying my life."

An almost indecipherably low response entered his mind.

"Are you sure, Ben? Because I'm pretty sure I saw you send all those texts. I'm also positive I saw you jerking off while thinking about Ryan. Maybe you don't know yourself very well, but I know you. And Cabin Green, as you so stupidly call it, isn't doing anything to destroy your life. You've already taken care of that well enough on your own, haven't you?"

"Shut up, shut up, shut up!" Ben pushed his fingers into his ears. "None of this is real. It's a grief-induced hallucination or a nightmare, but it's not real. Ghosts don't exist."

Trying his hardest to ignore the subtle whispers to the contrary, Ben glanced around for some normality. His eyes fell on the Marlboro case, and he gave into a strong nicotine craving. Sadness engulfed him as he considered the possibility that his friendship with Doug was over.

He would miss Mark and Stephen too, of course, along with Ryan – *who I did NOT sleep with* – but Doug had been his closest confidante for more than twenty years. The weight of this loss crushed the last bit of hope from his mind. He was also angry that any of his friends would believe such utter nonsense. They knew he was straight, so why would he have sex with Ryan?

CHAPTER THIRTY-TWO

Four Months Ago

"Hey guys, the little convenience story expanded. Not that it made much of a difference in their sales, apparently. I ran into a nice, chatty older guy, but aside from him and the cashier, there was no one else around. Oh, and they have a better beer selection now! Check out what I found," Stephen said as he held up two dusty twelve-packs of local brew.

"Nice!" Mark said.

Stephen flipped a beer bottle toward each of his friends. Doug and Mark cracked theirs open at the same time, sending a microscopic spray of amber liquid into the air. Ben hesitated for a second, running his finger down the side of the bottle. A clear trail was left in his finger's wake. "I wonder how long this has been sitting around?"

"It's really tasty, Ben," Doug reassured him.

"So, it's almost official! Our boy has become a man," Mark said to a chorus of laughter while patting Ben on the back. "I'd like to make a toast. Everyone, please raise your dusty beer bottles in honor of Ben and his lovely wife to be, Kyra."

All four bottles met with a resoundingly loud clink. The first toast was followed by two others, and Ben was soon a bit tipsy. He walked away from the group for a minute to take stock of how much his life was going to change.

This time next week, I'll be married. To Kyra. I must be the luckiest son of a bitch on the planet!

His fuzzy vision spotted something odd, but it took so long for his eyes to report the sighting to his brain that he had no idea what it actually was.

Must be drunker than I thought.

As Ben rejoined the group, Mark joked, "You're about to enter the next phase of your life. It's filled with a ball and chains, but not the fun kind. Your sex life is over, too, you know. I hope you are content to become celibate or perform 'drum solos' in secret."

Everyone else groaned at the male wedding clichés. "You know, Mark, I expect better of you. You're our resident funny man. Where's the originality?" Doug teased.

"Give me time, I'm just warming up."

This easy back and forth was par for the course with the group. Ben was the most reserved, but that didn't mean he failed to appreciate everyone else's extroverted nature: Mark, the jokester, Doug, with all his charisma, and Stephen, a naturally outspoken leader who didn't take anyone's shit. Meanwhile, Ben was the quiet thinker, and he guessed the other guys were still surprised someone with as much passion as Kyra had turned out to be his perfect match.

"I can't believe there's not going to be any strippers this weekend," Stephen said.

"If that really bums you out, I guess you could strip for us," Mark said. Before Stephen could respond, Mark continued, "I mean, don't. None of us wants to see that, not even Doug."

"There's not enough money in the world," Doug chimed in.

Stephen pretended to pout. "Are you sure? I think Ben would love it." He sauntered playfully over to Ben, pushed him into a sitting position and pretended to straddle him. "Get me some music, boys!"

Already laughing so hard he could barely breathe, Doug whipped out his iPhone and started a popular song from the eighties that had found new life blaring through the crappy sound system of every strip club in America. Mark and Doug encouraged Stephen to keep going with a series of catcalls and lewd commentary.

Ben turned a brighter shade of red by the second. It wasn't so much that Stephen was mock gyrating on his lap, but rather the fact that so much attention was aimed in his direction. It was always like this, though. His best friends had less inhibitions and were more comfortable doing just about anything in a social setting than Ben was, including making asses of themselves on purpose.

Truth be told, the future groom needed to blow off some steam, and the raucous laughter that always accompanied a trip to Cabin Green was exactly what the doctor ordered. He wasn't afraid of committing to one person. On the contrary, he was very much looking forward to it.

However, the idea of standing in front of a large group to make that commitment was terrifying.

Stephen was twirling his t-shirt over his head and performing the least sexy dance any of them had ever seen when Ben caught sight of something out of the corner of his eye. Turning his head to look directly at whatever it was didn't help. Again, he assured himself it was nothing more than the influence of alcohol.

How many drinks have I had? Four? Five?

Ben couldn't remember, but being a notorious lightweight meant anything more than two in a short timespan had the potential to leave him shitfaced. His bleary, disoriented view of the world informed him he couldn't trust his senses.

No one else seems to be seeing anything odd, so it must be all in my head, right?

The allure of embarrassing Ben, and himself, grew old for Stephen within ten minutes. Everyone held their stomach due to the strain of laughing so hard, but that didn't stop them from knocking back a few more beers.

"What now, buddy?" Doug asked.

Ben's mouth tasted stale from way too much alcohol, and he wanted a cigarette. His attempt at quitting was going well enough, but he figured the occasional smoke wasn't too big of a deal. Plus, this was a special occasion. He nodded toward the back door, and they all followed his lead.

As the guest of honor lit up, his bachelor party revelers got it into their drunk heads to make a bonfire. *That's probably not the best idea,* Ben mused.

It took the three guys an extended amount of time to get a fire going, but they did succeed eventually. It wouldn't have been a campfire without roasting marshmallows. Fortunately, aside from beer, the only other things Stephen had brought back from his supply run were a big bag of marshmallows and a package of hot dogs.

Priorities.

They spent the rest of the night around the bonfire, swapping stories and joking with Ben about his upcoming nuptials. They also managed to make their way through everything Stephen had bought earlier that day. Even Doug, who could drink multiple beers with as much ease as Popeye tossing back yet another can of spinach, became so intoxicated he started slurring his words.

* * * * *

None of them talked about it that day or later on, but Ben wasn't alone in seeing oddities. The others came to the same conclusion about it being nothing more than the side effect of alcohol, thereby making each sighting inconsequential.

Odd things continued happening after everyone sobered up, but no one ever saw anything head on. Who cared if some of their empty beer bottles seemed to change locations overnight? Each man reasoned they couldn't trust their memories of the night before, and this bought their silence.

CHAPTER THIRTY-THREE

Present Day

Ben was filled with the immensely strong sensation of being watched. This had been happening with greater frequency as each day passed, and he found it difficult to simply write it off as being connected to the ghost he didn't want to believe in.

A quick glance around the cabin showed him he was alone, at least in the physical sense, forcing him to admit once again that there was something supernatural afoot. When he made this concession, a mixture of terror and disbelief flooded his mind.

Naturally, as his flight or fight system engaged, his nicotine cravings kicked into higher gear than usual. Rationing had been ever tougher than he'd imagined. He hadn't gotten a proper dosage of nicotine in more than two days.

The headaches were beginning to set in, as were some mild stomach cramps. And it was only going to get worse.

Ben plopped down in front of the fireplace. The spectral fire had been extinguished, and the temperature in the cabin was dropping rapidly. He pulled a thin fleece blanket across his lanky frame, hiding the goosebumps that covered his arms.

"Now would be a good time for the fire trick," he said derisively.

The fireplace stayed dark, but the air around him turned colder than ice. He shivered as he pulled the blanket tighter. Every moment the temperature plunged another degree until the cabin air was well below the freezing mark.

His internal organs slowed down in response, much like a bear preparing for hibernation. He found it difficult to think. It soon became impossible to move without a concentrated struggle, so he resigned himself to lying on the floor, curled up into a ball in a futile attempt at keeping warm.

The temperature dropped so low that Ben's breath, which swirled around him in a white fog, became labored. Frost hardened the tips of his hair and eyebrows.

So, this is what it feels like to freeze to death.

It wasn't a pleasant way to go, but he was grateful for the almost instant numbness that had stolen over him. Ben wracked his brain for a way to save himself, but each thought that came to him involved being able to move. Lamentably, he was no longer able to even wiggle a toe. On the edge of giving up and giving into a horrible death, his mind latched on to a memory of Kyra.

CHAPTER THIRTY-FOUR

20 Months Ago

"What's wrong, sweetie?" Ben asked.

"I can't do it anymore, Ben. My boss is such a jerk," Kyra said.

Ben nodded, sympathetic to Kyra's plight. Her supervisor had made life difficult for as long as he'd known her. At times, the light in her eyes and smile had even gone out due to the bullish man's ridiculous demands.

Ben reached over and started massaging her shoulders and neck. "What happened this time?"

"The usual. He reamed me out in front of the entire office for something that was his fault, not mine."

"I'm sorry, hon."

"I wish this was a mere job instead of a career stepping stone. I want to quit so badly, but it could blacklist me for life."

"Hmmm... maybe a different type of solution is in order."

"Like what?"

The hope in her voice broke his heart because he didn't have any concrete ideas. "Well, I don't know. But I'm thinking whatever it is needs to be something outside the box."

The spark reignited in her hazel eyes. She kissed his cheek with gusto before grabbing her laptop.

"What are you doing?" Ben asked.

"Oh, you'll see." The mischievousness in her response left him excited, but also nervous. She had a level-headed approach to most things, but her feistiness threatened to get her into trouble sometimes.

"Let's see him squirm his way out of this one," she said.

"What did you do?"

"Exactly what you suggested; something outside the box." She elaborated with a satisfied giggle. "He's enough of a Don Draper from *Mad Men* wannabe to keep crude emails and videos on his work server, and I happen to know his log-in information."

"Wait... what does that mean?"

"I just 'accidentally' attached a file to a companywide email in his drafts. When he clicks send in the morning, he'll give the CEOs a viewing experience that's very much not-safe-for-work."

Stunned, Ben attempted to connect the dots between his loving girlfriend who always looked for the best in everyone and this revenge-seeking troublemaker.

"I did what you said, love. I thought outside the box to fix a problem much bigger than myself. You have no idea how many people he's hurt."

This was his first lesson about Kyra's darker underbelly. Although it made him uncomfortable at first, he later realized that her inconsistencies and darkness were an important part of the package.

The next day, Kyra's boss was suspended pending a review. Before the executive team finished with him, he had to face much worse problems than the video attachment he swore he didn't send. The only person blackballed by the entire incident was the one who truly deserved it. As Kyra liked to say, the good guys won for once.

CHAPTER THIRTY-FIVE

Present Day

I keep looking for a rational, easy way out of this. If Kyra was here, she'd look for the unconventional answer instead.

He glanced around for inspiration and was struck by a metaphorical light bulb.

I wonder. Well, there's no harm in trying, right?

"I'm sorry." Nothing happened, but the air around him become heavier.

"I shouldn't have used that tone of voice with you. I really am sorry," he said through chattering teeth.

A moment of silence passed. Ben almost gave up hope, but then the fire roared to life, bringing the temperature up at least ten degrees within five seconds. As each successive minute passed, Ben thawed out more. The frost was soon gone from his hair, and his extremities started to work again. With his teeth still slightly chattering, he said, "Th-thank you."

And thank you, Kyra.

No audible reply met his newfound gratitude, but the temperature continued to increase. Ben took this as a sign that the ghost had accepted his apology. He was aware how bizarre it was to be grateful to anyone or anything for reversing a terrible situation it had created. But he also knew he'd been on the verge of freezing to death. In this particular instance, the gratitude felt quite appropriate, regardless of the original source of his suffering.

As the last of the numbness was warmed away from his body, Ben contemplated what he'd just witnessed. If the ghost could be angered and appeased into acting out, could he figure out a way to convince it to let him go? If he undertook such a task, how big would the risk be?

Everything that had happened so far told him the ghost was keeping him locked away for a reason, but what if it just wanted someone to play with? *Could this all be nothing more than a sick game? Is there a way to leverage that to my advantage?* Maybe, just maybe, he could play a game, too, and end up winning his life back.

He had no way of knowing if it was even possible to win a game against a ghost, but he also knew he didn't have a whole lot of time left. Once the dwindling provisions ran out, he would soon cease to exist.

Unsure of how to address the ghost, he tentatively said, "Um... hello?" No one answered, but the air grew thicker again, which made him confident he had the spirit's attention.

"Um... the thing is... look, I obviously understand and respect your powers. You've demonstrated them to me, and they're extremely impressive. I was wondering if there was any way you could let me know why I'm being kept here? And also, if there might be a way for me to win my freedom?"

The last sentence ran out of Ben's mouth in a jumbled mess, but it was the best verbal delivery he could give while afraid for his life. The air around him paused, then the puzzle box levitated above the mantel. His eyes opened wide in fear and wonderment as the box floated across the air and came to a rest on the kitchen table. The lid slid off, and the pieces marched out of the box like little toy soldiers. One by one, they hurriedly clicked into place with a speed that a master puzzle builder could never have hoped to duplicate.

This time, the scene depicted on the puzzle contained only one of the two cars heading toward each other. He quickly tore his eyes from it and spun around in the kitchen chair.

A commanding voice tore through the air. "Watch the scene unfold, and then you may bargain for your soul."

Ben couldn't bear to accept this particular challenge and ran into the bedroom, slamming the door shut on the cackling of an apparently amused ghost. *Damn him!* There was nothing on this earth that was going to get him to watch that moment. He would just have to starve to death.

CHAPTER THIRTY-SIX

With a growling stomach and a tortured mind, Ben sat down upon the creaky old bed. They'd meant to replace the mattress, but getting a furniture delivery company to drive to such a remote location was challenging, even when they offered extra money. He glanced at his iPhone again, fearful of what he'd find, but desperate for a distraction. The battery had dwindled to two percent. "Well, I guess that's it."

The battery charger sat uselessly in the car, which might as well be a million miles away. He turned the phone over and over in his hands before his increasing lightheadedness caused him to drop his last bridge back to society.

"Shit."

Lowering himself to his haunches wasn't an appealing option, but he also didn't want to let the phone out of his sight. Never mind the fact that it wasn't doing him any good and only contained bad news. As

Ben got down closer to the floor, he was surprised to discover the smartphone wasn't as close as he'd expected.

It must have bounced under the bed.

He finished lowering himself into a flattened position. While retrieving the phone, Ben was startled by what looked like the shape of a human's face. He ordered himself to look at whatever it was more carefully. His first instinct was to use the flashlight on his phone, but with the battery almost dead, that wasn't a feasible solution. Although he hated the idea of expending energy, he decided to move the bed.

As the bed frame skidded across the floor, Ben saw it; the imprint of a human face. He did a double-take, half-convinced this was either a hallucination or a trick of the wood. No matter how many ways he looked at it, though, the face was clearly there. He continued to push the bed out of the way and uncovered a total of two faces. Without bothering to put the bed back, Ben sat down in stunned silence.

Were these always there? Was it some type of woodworking project? And if not, did this explain why he had the persistent feeling of being watched whenever he entered the bedroom? Could these faces have sentience?

All these questions made him queasy, and there were no easy answers. The only thing he knew to be true was if he didn't figure something out, and fast, this cabin was going to become his tomb.

* * * * *

Each day blended together. What could have been twenty-four hours or three weeks passed, and along with it went the majority of his food and all but one last hit on his final cigarette. The faces remained on the bedroom floor and had invited a few friends to join the macabre party; there were now seven of them. The puzzle continued to dominate the kitchen table, where it tortured him constantly by playing a soundtrack of squealing tires and screaming.

At one point, he'd tried to dismantle the puzzle, but this attempt burned his left pointer finger so badly that he needed medical attention. Since that wasn't an option, Ben had done his best to care for it himself. He was aware the finger would almost certainly be lost even if he miraculously got free. This particular display of power caused him to stop pleading with the ghost for clemency. Ben shifted his focus to sleeping, which conserved his waning energy and took away the puzzle's blaring horns.

His iPhone no longer worked, and he mourned its loss. Long gone was the ability to try in vain to reach out to others. Even worse, he no longer had the ability to listen to music; this loss hit him the hardest because he needed to find a way to drown out the puzzle's horrific noises. He was angered by the sabotage that kept him away from the phone's charger but didn't verbalize this feeling for fear of upsetting his spectral roommate.

In some ways, he even felt responsible. He was the one who had thought playing a game with a ghost might actually gain him his freedom. It was now clear he hadn't thought the plan through well enough to recognize a glaring gap in his reasoning. Ghosts might like to play, but this was undoubtedly because the odds would always be in their favor. Despite already having a tremendous advantage, this particular malevolent spirit expressed a clear predilection for playing dirty.

* * * * *

Ben struggled with his nicotine pangs for as long as he could, but his resolve finally dissolved into the insane cravings that go hand-in-hand with the side effects of withdrawal. He relit the stub waiting for him in the ashtray. Only one-and-a-half unsatisfying hits later, the last precious cigarette extinguished itself right at the edge of the filter.

He exhaled miserably and tried not to focus on the increasing horribleness of the withdrawal symptoms that were soon to come. He wasn't positive, but he thought he heard the slightest amount of snickering coming from the living room. It didn't surprise him in the least. If they were truly playing a game, it would only make sense to cheer on the weaknesses of the opposing team.

Knowing the cigarettes were gone made Ben's cravings more intense than ever. In despair, he gathered himself up and left the porch, shutting the door behind him. It was the first time he remembered closing the door that joins the living room and the enclosed patio since arriving at Cabin Green about three weeks ago. *Or was it three months?* The cabin's interior took on an even darker ambiance, but he hoped the 'out of sight, out of mind' principle would help curb some of his cravings.

Ben glanced toward the puzzle disdainfully. It roared to life in response. A big ball of tension knotted up inside his stomach, and he let loose an incoherent stream of yelling. Expressing some of his rage might have felt good, but it didn't convince the puzzle to stop. Instead, the volume increased until it drowned him out.

Ben put his hands over his ears while falling to his knees. The auditory sensory assault was too much to bear, and his body rocked back and forth. He was no longer sure he was strong enough to withstand the game he'd foolishly joined, but he couldn't bring himself to utilize the alternative. He was aware watching the puzzle unfold would lead to his salvation, but he feared doing so would also be the straw that broke the back of his fading sanity. Of course, not doing so would soon cause him to starve to death. Neither option was palatable, but for the moment, he chose to maintain his present course.

His hunger rivaled the knots in his stomach, so he dragged himself back up into a standing position and shuffled into the kitchen. The supplies were almost gone. Ben had been carefully rationing the food, but it had lasted for even less time than he'd anticipated. By midday tomorrow, he would be out of food, regardless of how much he tried to stretch his meager supplies.

CHAPTER THIRTY-SEVEN

After deplaning and hopping into a taxi, Doug noticed the policeman was right; Virginia Beach was lovely this time of year. He and Ryan would've probably had a good time here if this was a vacation as opposed to a search mission.

They started their day at the resort Ben had spoken so highly of. Everything he said was true, too. There were multiple sparkling pools, a tennis court, an elaborate spa located off the lobby, beach access, and much more. The couple noted these two things unconsciously, but neither was in the mood to be impressed by vacation amenities.

Striding up to the front desk, Doug surreptitiously glanced at every lanky male with dark hair in the general vicinity. Saddened that none of them were Ben, he launched into an explanation as soon as he reached the front desk clerk. The clerk exhibited a proper amount of sympathy but cautioned he wouldn't be able to reveal much due to the resort's rules about privacy.

"Ah, here we are. Well, the good news is I can tell you everything I know. The bad news is this consists solely of the fact that your friend never checked in."

"Do you mean he was a no-show?"

"No, nothing like that. He was responsible enough to contact our reservations department more than twenty-four hours before his anticipated arrival time. We canceled his reservation and refunded the holding fee since he gave us ample notice. I'm afraid that I have no idea where he is, but I sure hope you find him. Maybe he ended up staying at a different local resort, but the notes do indicate that he said he was canceling his trip to Virginia Beach altogether."

Stunned, Doug could barely choke out a "thank you" before walking away. The mystery of what happened to Ben kept getting deeper and more intricate. He wondered if this was one of those situations where someone finds out that they didn't know the inner workings of the other person's mind at all. He dismissed this notion almost as quickly as it popped up, but a new fear seized his heart; could Ben have decided to kill himself? The mere thought caused trickles of anxiety sweat to appear all over his body.

Doug promised himself he'd utilize the next two days to look for clues about Ben's disappearance before allowing his thoughts to go down such a dark and painful path. It kept nagging at him, though, and his mind seemed to be slowly unraveling an idea about Ben's possible whereabouts. The sensation was similar to having something on the tip of your tongue but being unable to remember it.

It'll come to me.

A little later, he added a mental prayer: *Please come to me in time.*

CHAPTER THIRTY-EIGHT

The last crumbs of food had been ingested, and the incessant noises from the puzzle had escalated to such a din that they infiltrated everything, including Ben's dreams. He had given up on taking dream-suppressing sleeping pills because they made him feel sick when taken on an empty stomach.

Nothing he tried brought any relief, and he began to reassess his options. Death versus watching the puzzle no longer seemed like a cut and dry decision. His starved mind mused over how amazing it was that hunger and fatigue could alter one's convictions.

The idea of giving into the ghost was both terrifying and seductive. It could mean his release. Or it could be nothing more than an awful trick that would leave him mentally destroyed and still on the path of starving to death. What should he choose? This decision was the most complicated one of Ben's life, and it wasn't made any easier by the constant pain of withdrawal that wracked his body.

As he contemplated the pros and cons of each choice, a wave of nausea overtook him. He barely made it to the toilet before letting lose the last remnants of sustenance within his stomach. He'd been vomiting off and on for almost half a day now, and no amount of water seemed able to keep him hydrated.

With a half-hearted attempt at washing out his mouth completed, he stumbled back through the cabin before shutting himself into the bedroom. The room had taken on the desolate, repressive connotations of a prison cell.

Ben longed for the release of the outdoors. The rest of the cabin was too sinister to reside in for long. Against his better judgment, he'd resorted to spending most of the last week within this tiny space, despite it being almost too small to fit the lumpy, full-sized bed.

Ben plopped himself on the mattress and tried to think of something that could temporarily override the hunger and pain that gnawed at him like a famished dog with a newfound bone. He also studiously avoided looking at the floor. Every inch now contained a face, and many of them appeared to be screaming.

The struggle to keep memories at bay occupied his mind, as did the bitter battle between his own opposing points of view. There was one bright light offering a beacon of hope in the bitter darkness; for the first time in weeks, his dreams offered a much-needed respite from his suffering. Rather than suffocating him with fearful imagery, his sole form of escape now took him back in time to moments he'd shared with Kyra.

* * * * *

Hours later, Ben awoke to a painfully empty stomach. Some of the mental cobwebs had cleared, but they soon came back with reinforcements. As he attempted to hold the threads of his sanity together, he heard something wondrous. Cocking his head to the side, he waited for confirmation that his mind wasn't simply playing tricks on him.

There it is again!

A rush of strength and hope enabled him to leap from the bed. He ran on stumbling feet toward the front door, where he rested his head on the wood and prayed the sound would come one more time.

The strong rattling against his ear was proof; someone was knocking on the door! Even better, the broken doorknob had somehow reattached itself!

With wild abandon, his hand darted to the knob and tested it tentatively. It turned. A lopsided grin moved his lips in an upward direction for the first time in days. The tension in his face threatened to crack his flesh in half at the unexpected request for elasticity, but he couldn't have been more overjoyed.

In stunned silence, he listened as the man on the other side of the door frame pleaded for assistance.

"Oh, thank god! I need some help, fella. I... wait. I know you! Aren't you the young man from the Dash-n-Save parking lot?"

Not trusting his mouth to form actual words, Ben nodded in agreement.

"I had a car accident about a half-a-mile away. Damn deer ran straight into my front bumper. I can't get a signal on this piece of crap phone. I've been wandering 'round hoping to find someone."

Ben had never been so excited – or excited at all, truth be told – by the sight of protruding ear hair. This man and his well-timed accident would be his salvation. Or would he? Tendrils of doubt licked at the corners of his mind.

There's no way it's going to let me leave. Or him. We're both screwed now. The elderly man looked at him expectantly, and he realized he must have zoned out for a second.

"I'm sorry, what was that?"

"I said, can you please give me a ride, sonny? To the Dash-n-Save?"

"Yes," Ben said with a questioning lilt and an imperceptible glance from side to side. When the darkness didn't advance upon him or do something less subtle, such as cause the walls to start dripping blood, he spoke again with more vigor. "YES!"

The slightest hesitation was filled with one question – *should I grab my stuff?* – and the instantaneous internal response – *NO!* If he was ever going to break free of this wretched cabin, the moment had to be now. Grabbing his keys, he rushed outside and darted toward the Honda Civic.

"Don't you want to lock up?" the man asked.

"Uh, it's fine. It, uh, locks on its own."

"Is that right? I need to look into that. I'm always forgetting to lock doors. I reckon I'm probably too old to drive, too, but I won't stop 'til they pry the keys out of my hands," he laughed.

Ben failed to take in most of the elderly man's idle chatter, but the sound of another person's voice almost caused him to weep. His primary concern was reaching the main road. Fearful he'd suffer a repeat of the last time he attempted to leave, he focused all his attention on the twisty path ahead.

The sweet crunching sound that accompanied the Honda's tires as they turned from the rock covered path to the concrete road made his heart leap. A mere ten miles was all that stood between him and civilization. If they could make it that far, he'd never have to see Cabin Green, or its resident ghosts, ever again.

It's going to work! I can't believe it's this easy. Why the hell wasn't I able to leave before?

He stayed silent on the drive to the Dash-n-Save. There was nothing he could say that would make sense to his elderly companion, nor could he ask to borrow a useless phone that was far out of signal range. Driving was his sole option now.

His pulse quickened as he saw the first lights of the tiny town. He was really here. This horrible situation was about to end. Jamming the car into park, his muscles tensed at the expectation of throwing himself toward the convenience store. Inside there would be cigarettes, a phone, and food!

As the man exited Ben's car, he looked at him quizzically. "Say, are you all right, son? You seem a bit... I don't know, anxious?"

He opened his mouth to speak, but his vocal chords and lips conspired against him. In his mind, Ben said, *No, I'm not all right. I need help now. Please help me.* What his ears reported him saying was something entirely different.

"That's kind of you to ask, sir, but I assure you, I'm doing great!"

"Okay, then... well, thanks again for your help. Say, can I interest you in a pack of smokes for your trouble?"

Oh my god, yes. A million times yes. Cigarettes, then a phone. Get me out of this hell!

"That's not necessary, sir. I've got a pack here in my pocket and a couple of cartons at the cabin."

Infuriated with his self-betrayal, Ben tried to force his voice, or at least his face, to signal the man that he was being held hostage by an evil spirit. None of his efforts were fruitful, though, and the man bid him farewell. Left to his own devices, Ben ordered his body to leave the vehicle. Yet again, his command was ignored completely, and his right hand shifted the car into reverse.

NO. Stop it, goddammit!

Against his will, he drove the car back the way he'd come. Repeated attempts at veering off course were squashed by an insistent presence that forbid him from enacting his own will. Exhausted from the sheer effort of trying to break free, he soon stumbled back into the cabin.

With a definitive click, the door locked him back inside. A beat later, a loud clunk got his attention. He turned back around, fearful of what the sound meant. His eyes lingered on the proof that his trepidation was well-founded; the doorknob laid uselessly on the floor again.

CHAPTER THIRTY-NINE

Rose sat behind the entrance desk at Banks Psychiatric Care with the telephone pressed to her ear. The phone rang five times before it went to voicemail.

Hi, this is Ben. Leave a message, and I'll get back to you as soon as possible.

Frustrated, she hung up without saying anything. A young female co-worker said, "Still no answer?"

"No," Rose replied with a deep sigh.

"You've been trying to get a hold of him for what... three weeks now?"

"Give or take a day, yeah."

"Wasn't the funeral last week?"

Rose nodded. "It just doesn't seem right to stop trying to reach him. I mean, I've met Ben before. He loves his mother. None of this makes any sense. I hope there's nothing wrong with him..."

"Is it true, what the nurses said?"

"I don't know. What did they say?"

Rose's co-worker squirmed a bit before answering.

"Some of them swear she died of fright. They said it was like she'd seen a ghost or something."

Rose contemplated this question. Her eyebrows scrunched together and the slightest hint of tears appeared in her eyes. She'd known Sara Tremblay for several years, and it was hard to not get attached to a long-term patient.

"The autopsy said she died from a heart attack, but honestly? I really don't know what to believe," Rose said. "All I know for sure is that I heard her screaming 'take me instead' right before she died."

CHAPTER FORTY

Losing his one opportunity to escape left Ben despondent; he was heartbroken, starving, and desperate for nicotine. Isolation had also grabbed a firmer hold on his psyche than before, leaving him a fractured mess. All he wanted was a way out that didn't threaten to leave him in even worse shape.

Starvation-induced hallucinations became the norm, and the laws of time changed in response to his dire condition. The clock now moved forward in strange leaps and bounds. He frequently found himself engaged in actions that made no sense at all without any memories of the moments that preceded each action.

It was like being a strung-out insomniac. Time stuttered and shifted around him without any respect to the laws of physics. Life soon became a serious of confounding snapshots.

Click.

He was lying on the floor with his hair shorn off and scattered everywhere. The electric razor still hummed in his right hand. Looking at it in shock, he tossed it aside while curling up into the sitting version of a ball. *Oh my god. What did I just do?*

Click.

Ben cut one of his dirty t-shirts into several small scraps, which he then attempted to fit over the puzzle's individual pieces. His efforts were for naught, as he quickly discovered he could somehow still see the pieces through the dark-colored shirt. Like that wasn't bad enough, the shirt scraps soon gave up the charade of even attempting to get the job done. They mocked him through levitation, which left more than enough room to see the puzzle scene depicted below.

He squeezed his eyes shut, fearful of what would come next. When nothing happened during a single moment that stretched out forever, he took a risk by opening one eye. The puzzle stared back at him, exactly as he'd left it, but the t-shirt scraps were nowhere to be seen.

Click.

He rocked and sobbed on the bed. Even after everything he'd been through, Ben still found it hard to believe the three dark shapes around him had a paranormal origin.

I'm just like my mom. None of this is real. Wake up. Wake up. WAKE UP!

Sneaking a glance at his tormentors, he noted once again that no amount of self-admonishment made any difference. The darkness surrounded him, and there was still a part of his brain that insisted he'd been dealing with the spirit world, not a mental illness.

Maybe that's what she thought too.

Click.

He hugged the toilet as wave after wave of nausea wracked his body. Although he didn't remember it, Ben had no doubt that he'd been kneeling on the bathroom floor for quite some time. He no longer had any food in his system, so the nausea was repeatedly expressed with nothing more than stomach acid.

He'd reached a state of complete misery akin to having every hangover of his life combined into one, but Ben intuitively understood this might be the best place for him. Vomiting, or at least attempting to, kept the dark shapes and other mental tricks at bay.

Or maybe they really are ghosts and this grosses them out. Perhaps they're even demons?

Click.

His wrists were slashed open, and the brilliantly red blood swirled down the bathroom sink. Ben stifled his sobs as the sweet mercy and sense of calmness took over in response to the faltering of his heartbeat. As the last remaining piece of energy and hope abandoned him, he lost his footing and fell to the ground, grateful for his upcoming death.

His eyes clouded over, and he allowed his head to come to rest on the wall right next to the water pipes. He prepared for a premature death and wasn't surprised to learn that the sensation of his life draining away made him more uplifted than he'd been in months.

Click.

Ben's eyelids were forced open and a dark fog surrounded his face.

"You will not do this," a voice bellowed into his ears with such intensity that it caused his bowels to shake. "Look," it commanded, and his eyes drifted down to his wrists. The wounds were tended to by unseen hands.

"What?" he asked incredulously.

"That would be cheating."

"But I thought you wanted me to die."

"Not before you understand."

His body inflated as the blood he'd lost shot up out of the drain and injected itself into his closing wounds. Ben's heart and other vital organs reached out greedily for the life-giving fluid while his body refilled to capacity. Once the process was complete, he blacked out and spent the next several hours lying on the bathroom floor.

* * * * *

Ben stiffly sat up and his bones cracked. He conducted a quick visual inspection of himself and the sink. There were no residual traces of any blood, but he did have thin, white scars tracing his veins.

The ghost might have set him right, at least by its own reckoning, but it'd also left him with the proof of his failed attempt. He wondered if this has been done on purpose, or if there'd been no way to prevent it. He leaned strongly toward the former option.

If the ghost, or whatever the hell it is, can restore blood and seal wounds, you can be damn sure it could've gotten rid of these ugly scars. It wants me to be marked. It wants me to remember.

The most significant thing about what had transpired untold hours ago was it had shown him the true power of his enemy. Not only could he not leave the cabin but he also couldn't exercise enough free will to take his own life There was no white flag, and there wouldn't be any mercy. He had to play the spirit's game until the end, regardless of his own thoughts about the matter.

Grief twisted Ben's face as he looked at himself in the mirror. What the image reflected back was shocking; he'd become bald, bruised, and horribly emaciated. He mourned the loss of his hair for a second, only half-remembering the circumstances under which he'd rid himself of it.

Nothing about his time at the cabin made much sense, but the last four or five days had been a spectacularly awful roller coaster ride into the depths of Hell. There'd been a countless list of unimaginable trials, which he'd grown certain existed solely to test his endurance. There was only one left now that counted, and it might allow him to gain his freedom. He had to go into the dining room and watch the entire puzzle scene.

It was easy enough to understand this requirement, but Ben found it impossible to wrap his mind around doing it. Surely, following the ghost's lead would only lead to a new form of madness. What possible good could come from it?

In answer to his unspoken question, the spirit whispered into his ear. "It could set you free."

Ben jumped at the harsh, grating sound of his tormenter. It still surprised him whenever it spoke, and he doubted anyone could ever get used to the sound of it. In fact, the voice delivered its own unique form of torture; the dissonant noise caused his insides to tremble and his hands to shake, regardless of the content of the entity's taunts.

"No. Please, God, no."

"Don't be such a child," the ghost taunted him. "There is no God to save you, and I can keep this up forever. Can you?"

He didn't respond with words, but fresh tears sprang from his eyes. Ben had reached the end, and he knew it. His stomach was far into the process of ravaging itself, and there wasn't enough body fat left for it to go on much longer. His mind teetered on the precipice of complete and utter madness. He seemed destined to fall regardless of which choice he made.

He wanted a cigarette more than anything else on earth. Half-laughing to himself, he realized he would be more willing to make a deal with the devil for a cigarette than for a way out of the cabin. *How pathetic.* Ben wondered how disappointed Kyra would have been to see him become such a frail husk of his former self. Maybe he had never really been as strong as he'd believed. Maybe no one ever was.

CHAPTER FORTY-ONE

As they flew home, Doug ruminated over how useless the trip to Virginia Beach had been. He and Ryan hadn't found a single clue to help them locate their missing friend. And now, they were headed back to a world that expected each of them to report to work in the morning. Ryan would do exactly that, but the idea of slipping into the persona of a caring real estate agent was more than Doug could bear.

Sighing, he sneaked a glance at the sleeping form of his husband. The small light above their seats lit up Ryan's smooth, dark skin.

The last two days had been an exhausting whirlwind, so it was no surprise that Ryan was fast asleep. Envious, Doug tried to formulate the next phase of his plan. He would gladly search the ends of the earth for his lifelong friend, but first, he needed to figure out where to go next.

There was still something gnawing at the back of his mind, but despite his best efforts to retrieve it, the information remained elusive.

Where are you, Ben?

CHAPTER FORTY-TWO

The struggle to decide between facing up to the past or dying left Ben in shambles. Being partially paralyzed for several hours at a time – one of his latest negative developments - was the least of his worries. Living without movement is one thing, but having his organs shut down was a one-way ticket. He could no longer expel any waste or do anything else other than dry heave.

His body rejected the water he tried to force into it. His lips were cracked and bloody, his skin had turned ashen, and a mephitic stink permeated the air. A new level of cold had also introduced itself. Constant shivering gave way to desperation as his temperature dove to new, impossible lows. Ben understood that these things meant his physical and mental death drew near.

His starved mind grasped on to the idea that this deep level of suffering provided proof humans don't have a soul. This seemed like the only conceivable explanation for why it hurt so damn much to feel his life draining away.

He rationalized if there was a soul, and if it was destined to soon be released to a better place, he should be looking forward to death rather than trying to find a way to stave it off. Maybe there was more to man's fight or flight instincts than any scientist or theologian wanted to admit.

Ben wondered if the most devoted men of the cloth had such revelations while lying upon their death beds. Or did they know a secret way to silence the urge to live? Either way, he imagined they must have been utterly disappointed in their last seconds of life as they realized there was no tunnel of light and no pearly gates. He empathized with them, for he now had a pretty good idea what it felt like to waste one's life in the pursuit of something that would never come to fruition.

All he had wanted was a life with Kyra. Even if he survived this experience, that future would forever be denied to him. This left him searching deep inside of himself for an override switch. Part of his psyche might not have been ready to die yet, but the rest of him wanted it to be. As Ben's mind connected with such deep-reaching concepts, he was greeted by the unpleasant sight of his own personal ghost.

Its darkness floated in and out of the bedroom on a regular basis and checked to see if he was still breathing. It became clear the ghost was as determined to break him as Ben was to resist its efforts. Numerous times he'd woken up and found the darkness practically swallowing him whole. These encounters made him distinctly uncomfortable and lowered his diminished body temperature by at least another degree. But he wasn't harmed in any visible way.

Regardless of the lack of physical wounds, he wondered if the ghost was in some way responsible for his scattered thoughts and lack of decisiveness. Just as he would decide to let himself go, he would feel stricken by the strongest desire to hold on to his life and would almost tear himself from the bed and run to the puzzle. In those moments, he had to physically restrain himself, and this was getting harder and harder to do as his limbs grew weaker by the moment.

He spoke to the ghost several times in an increasingly faltering voice. "This is so unfair. What did I do to deserve this?"

The evil specter never verbally responded to such statements, but it did remind him at least five times a day that he only had to do one thing to bring all of this to an end. Ben continued to respond to this information the same way: shaking his head no, followed by bearing down against another wave of nausea, chills, and pain.

* * * * *

Ben had become too weak to leave the bed, even for a drink of water, and the incessant dehydration plaguing him became far worse. All his flesh was cracking open, and at times he'd resorted to licking up his own blood in a desperate attempt to moisten his mouth. It was now as dry as sandpaper, and he could no longer swallow without feeling like he was going to choke to death.

"Darkness," he whispered out.

It came for him swiftly, filling the room almost completely with the enormity of its size. "Yes?" it asked.

"Water," Ben sputtered.

It laughed at him.

"Water, then the puzzle," he rasped out.

It considered him for a moment before leaving the room. Soon, a pitcher of water materialized on the bedside table. Ben didn't have the strength to lift it. He dunked his mouth into the pitcher and drank a bountiful amount, over half of which he vomited on the floor less than thirty seconds later. Ben was now more wretched than ever, with a pounding head and a sore throat that was almost certainly soaked in blood rather than water.

The ghost watched Ben deal with the bitterness of receiving hydration several hours past the time when it had become a critical need. It knew the man was going to undergo some serious cramping and discomfort, and it decided to stick around to see how its prey would handle this latest trial.

Ben no longer beheld the presence of the ghost as he attempted to live past the agonizing moments that followed. Every muscle in his body cramped, and he began dry heaving again. The water had tasted brilliant, but he'd obviously far overdone it. He promised himself he would tread more carefully with his next drink.

Several minutes later, the worst of the cramping passed, along with the dry heaves. He took a couple of deep breaths to prepare himself, then contemplated getting another drink. Before he could move toward it, the pitcher rose into the air, far out of his reach.

"It's time," the ghost said.

He faltered for a moment, eyeing the water and thinking over his choices. With a tone of fear, he said, "No."

The darkness swelled all around Ben as disembodied screams and shrieks pierced his eardrums. He covered his ears in a futile attempt to block out some of the noise while remembering what it had been like to go without his hearing. He prayed he wasn't about to lose it again.

The pitcher of water shattered against the far wall, soaking into the wood without leaving a single drop behind. Everything aside from Ben and the bed rocked in place before being lifted up into the air. A lamp, a dresser, and the bedside table all collided above him, then fell on top of his body with a sickening crunch. Ben gasped out in pain as his limbs went numb. Blood seeped from every orifice. As he slipped into what he was certain would be his final sleep, Ben managed to lift the corners of his mouth up into a slight smile. He'd angered the ghost enough to win; he would never again have to see the scene within the puzzle.

While drifting unconscious, Ben felt the life leaving his body. He was happy to have received this fate in exchange for the one the ghost had prepped him for. He wondered what the evil entity would do now and if his body would survive long enough for any of his friends to come across his carcass. It didn't matter, though, as long as he was free of the cabin.

The sensation of floating in space jarred him. Ben had vacillated so much during the past three-and-a-half months with matters of faith that he was in shock at being this close to receiving an answer. The floating made him think of the so-called white tunnel some people reported seeing after living through a near death experience, and it brought with it a considerable level of anxiety.

If there was a Heaven and Hell, he was surely headed for the wrong place. He found himself hoping it would be as desolate and horrible as the puzzle world that kept replaying itself in his mind. Before he could learn anything definitive about the eventual fate of mankind, he became aware of his body again.

The blackness had swept through the room, removed everything from his body, and tossed the broken shards of furniture into the corner. It surrounded Ben's frame more tightly than it had in the past, and instead of making him colder, it somehow brought warmth to his bones. This unexpected, life-giving heat caused his eyelids to flutter and his mind to stop wandering. He was going to live, dammit. He would be forced to return to playing the ghost's game.

CHAPTER FORTY-THREE

Ben had hit the end of his proverbial rope. Another twenty-four hours, give or take a few, had passed since his death was so rudely interrupted for the second time in less than a week. He could no longer sense his own body, and his eyes reported everything back to him in triplicate. He would have called to the ghost for assistance, but there was no way it would believe him again. In lieu of an easier answer, he shifted his body, inch by inch, toward the edge of the bed.

More than an hour later, Ben realized he'd moved less than six inches and let his head flop back on the mattress, exhausted. Sweat laced his vision, and as it cooled, it added to the chill that had consumed his frame for the past several hours. He wanted to give up on giving up but knew there was no alternative. After a few minutes rest, he began the process anew.

He finally managed to make it out of bed, landing with a thud on the floor. Fortunately, the ghost had left the bedroom door open after its last tirade. Ben was now lying across the threshold. His eyes fluttered over to the kitchen table, and he was distressed to see it appeared to be miles away. He had to make it, though, no matter how arduous the journey.

It had become apparent the ghost wouldn't let him die until he completed this one last task. He no longer wanted to go home; he simply wanted to be given the freedom to die. It was enough to push him forward.

He moved slowly across the floor, chasing the beams of sunlight as they worked their way throughout the cabin, signaling the beginning and then the end of yet another day. Somewhere during the course of the first day, he shut out all thoughts of what he was crawling toward as a means of keeping his limbs moving. He agonizingly achieved less than an inch at a time as his body struggled to respond to his mental commands.

Ben's body and mind longed to shut down, but the ability to do so had been blocked somehow by the resident ghost of this now much-hated cabin. He made a pact with himself; if he did get out of this alive, his first act would be to burn Cabin Green to the ground. It might have been irrational, but he'd become adamant the cabin itself was as much to blame for his woes as the ghost was. If the opportunity arose, he was determined to punish Cabin Green for its role in his personal Hell.

* * * * *

The ghost's attention was piqued when Ben managed to crawl within five feet of the table. It appeared the human was going to give in and play the game, but the entity was experienced enough in these matters to know it couldn't count on anything until it actually happened. To prevent the man from being scared off at the last second, it made sure to silence any noises coming from the puzzle.

It relocated its own presence outside of the man's current view and waited to see what would happen next. To its continual surprise, this man named Ben kept plodding forward. Aware this was a precarious moment, it lowered the room's temperature by five degrees, thus announcing its presence. There was also a sense of decorum in this decision; the cooler air dried some of the foul sweat that clung to all parts of the man's body.

Humans are so disgusting.

Centuries had passed since the entity had held a physical form for more than an hour at a time. This had removed any empathy it might have once possessed. When it looked at the body crawling across the floor, it had no sense of internal recognition. All it felt was a severe distaste for the entire human race.

The long passage of time rendered the ghost unable to imagine why and how it'd ever once allowed itself to be encased for decades in a human form. The fallible confines of flesh and bone were a prison.

These ingrates should be begging for a quick end rather than trying to bargain to extend their pathetic existence.

It had heard every imaginable request and demand spoken from people in various states of despair. None had ever been quite as intriguing as this particular human, though. It had been right to pick him so long ago. The ghost hovered at rapt attention waiting for the outcome of several different possible conclusions.

Don't let me down again.

* * * * *

Ben endured another hour of crawling forward upon scraped up knees and elbows before reaching his destination. He looked up at the chair's seat and was flooded with anguish. How was he supposed to get on it? It seemed impossible, and he despondently thought he'd wasted all his time and energy trying to achieve an unreachable goal.

Before letting himself slip too deeply down the darkened recesses of his mind, he laid his head down upon the ground. *I just need to rest for a bit. Then I can do this.*

His moment of rest turned into several hours as he slipped deep into the nether regions of sleep once again. By the time he awoke, the sun was beating down upon the cabin. Shafts of light illuminated his emaciated frame as thousands of tiny dust particles danced through the air.

Ben gritted his teeth and put his arms out toward his final destination. The chair was harsh and unforgiving underneath his weakened hands, but he somehow willed his fingers into curling around the wood. He used the stabilizing force of the chair to his advantage and pulled himself up into an almost sitting position on the floor. The effort soaked his back and face with fresh sweat. All that was left now was to pull himself up onto the seat of the chair; then he'd be able to rest for good.

Several ineffective attempts found him sliding back to the ground, but he refused to give up after having come so far. He repeatedly struggled into a kneeling position before succeeding at wrapping his arms around the back of the chair. The empty seat mocked Ben with its closeness. Numerous failed attempts caused him to hurt his knees and arms, but he achieved a momentous goal by hoisting his stomach onto the seat. Dizziness grab on to his body and mind.

The only response that made sense was to close his eyes and beg the earth to stop spinning. The world spun beneath him for longer than his protein-deprived mind could comprehend, but the dizziness eventually receded enough for him to move again.

Ben's arms reached out for the top of the back of the chair, and his hands took the firmest hold possible upon the wood. He half-pulled, half-shimmied his body upward until, with a resounding feeling of success, he found himself sitting on the chair.

Ben's neck could no longer remain upright under the strain of his head. His shoulders rolled forward until his exhausted head came to rest on the kitchen table. He passed out yet again, mere inches from his goal.

When he came to, the darkness was occupying the space in front of him. It looked at him with an almost human-like curiosity as it tried to determine if Ben was going to go through with his task.

He glared at the ghost, wishing it would allow him to look into the puzzle alone, but knowing there had never been a chance of that happening. His torturer was too invested in seeing the outcome; there was no way it was going to miss the big payoff of its extended period of work. No matter what its prey wanted, the darkness was determined to savor every last drop of the human's fear and sadness.

The two combatants looked at each other, neither speaking nor moving for several moments before the ghost broke the silence.

"Are you ready?"

Ben glanced down at the puzzle, which was currently one solid color, then brought his eyes up to meet the gaze of his tormenter. "Yes." His voice did not falter as it delivered his answer, and he was surprised to discover he was telling the truth.

"There are a few rules. Once the scene starts, you must watch it until the very end. If you do not, you'll have to start over from the beginning. Do you understand?"

Ben gloomily nodded his head. There was no way he wanted to see any of this more than once, so he ordered himself to see it all the way through the first time, no matter what. It was time to get this over with and move on to the glorious release of death that would undoubtedly follow the viewing party.

Ben laughed at himself over the morbidity of using the word 'party' to explain what was happening, while reflecting on the incredible adaptive ability of human beings. Even with everything he'd been through, he had still summoned the strength to face what he'd once feared more than anything else.

The air around him seemed palpable; not just with tension but like the cabin itself was alive and waiting for the results of the upcoming minutes. The darkness filled almost all the otherwise unoccupied space of air opposite Ben, and he still had the sensation of being watched from other directions.

Perhaps encounters like this were akin to watching television for ghosts and others had been invited to watch the final act. This was a disturbing thought, but he wasn't going to let it distract him from his goal. All he had to do was watch the puzzle unfold one time, from beginning to end. Then he could finally be at peace.

CHAPTER FORTY-FOUR

Doug awoke with a start.

What was that?

As wakefulness began to enter his brain, he realized his phone had beeped. Trying hard not to get his hopes up, he reached for the iPhone and quickly scanned the screen. There it was! A voicemail icon. No one would leave a message this late at night unless it was important or an emergency, right?

His hands fumbled to press the phone icon. At first, Doug's chest fell as he realized the caller was identified as 'No Caller ID.' In the past, he would've rolled back over and resumed sleeping without bothering to press play, but tonight was a big exception. He'd exhausted all means of finding Ben, so with trepidation, he clicked the play icon.

Static. It was nothing but static.

What kind of prank is this?

Just as he began to pull the phone from his ear, Doug heard the slightest hint of a voice. "...oug, it's... n." A long period of static followed with his heart pounding and a palpable taste of fear rising in his throat. "...in Gre..."

He listened to the message four times before putting the pieces together. "Holy crap. Cabin Green? He's at Cabin Green?!?"

"Wha...?" mumbled Ryan, who had been snoring next to Doug for the past few hours.

"It's Ben! A voicemail from Ben. Cabin Green!" Doug jumped out of bed and tossed on random clothes.

"Ben?" Ryan's voice weakly answered. After a second, his husband's words sunk into his half-asleep mind. "Wait, Ben called? And what did you say, he's at Cabin Green?"

"Yes!" Doug said while shoving a few quick items into a duffel bag.

"What are you doing?"

"I have to go find him, hon. The message was really weird. He could still be in trouble."

"Yes, of course, but right now? It's, what, a little past midnight? And Cabin Green is six hours away. You need to get some sleep."

"I can't. I don't know how to explain it, but I know I have to get there as soon as possible. I'll be fine. I'm beyond wired now anyway, and I did take a nap earlier today. I know you can't get another day off work, but I can. I'll go find him, get him help if needed, and be back within a day or two. Okay?"

Ryan's eyes were darkened by anxiety, but he had a difficult time saying no to Doug about anything, especially something that meant this much to him.

"Okay, babe," he acquiesced. "But please promise me something."

"Anything."

"Let me know when you get there and pull over if you start to get sleepy. Getting yourself killed isn't going to help Ben, and I'm way too young to be a widow," he half-heartedly laughed.

"I'll be fine, I promise. And thank you for your support. You're the best, Ryan. I love you so freaking much."

The two embraced for a long moment, followed by a loving kiss. As they began to pull apart, both men stopped to look into each other's eyes. There was fear and mistiness in each set, but neither tried to change the plans that had been set in motion.

Doug packed a few more necessities and gave his husband another hug and kiss. Then his big truck barreled down I-75 North at almost fifteen miles-per-hour above the posted limit of seventy.

"I'm coming, buddy," he said in a thin, whispery voice that betrayed his lack of confidence. Although he told Ryan the truth when he said he had to go right away, he didn't tell him how afraid he was of what he'd find.

CHAPTER FORTY-FIVE

Ben rested his hands on the table in an effort to brace himself from what was soon to come. He nodded his agreement to the ghost's terms and issued a silent command to the puzzle. It instantly sprang to life. As he'd dreaded, it was a scene taken from his actual life, but it surprised him by beginning much earlier than he'd predicted. He was somehow being shown things from a perspective that he hadn't actually had.

The scene started in Kyra's living room. She was on the phone with him finalizing their plans for that evening. Confronted with her beauty, he sucked in a harsh, jagged breath. She was even more brilliant than his memory had rendered her. Tears sprang into the corners of Ben's eyes as her melodious voice said, "I love you," before clicking end on her cellphone.

She walked gracefully to the hallway mirror and gave herself a quick glance. Ben thought everything about her was perfect, but she spotted a couple of things that brought a hint of a frown to her face. She quickly set about fixing her makeup before plucking a couple of stray eyebrow hairs.

Finally satisfied, Kyra went into the entry closet and selected a lightweight, dark brown jacket. The summer weather was warm, but it was also damp out, so she thought a coat might become necessary later in the evening. Kyra slipped on her shoes, put the coat over her left arm, and picked up her keys with a jingle that caught the attention of her youngest cat. She stooped down to the feline's level and scratched her behind the ears.

"I'll be back in a few hours, Mephi," she said before giving her a quick kiss on the forehead. With the cat momentarily placated, Kyra straightened up and made her way to the front door. She picked up an umbrella as an afterthought, crossed the door's threshold, and locked the deadbolt.

She barely glanced around as she traipsed across the parking lot. Slipping into her car, she noticed that the predicted storm clouds were indeed gathering off in the not too distant sky.

Good call on the umbrella. And the new wiper blades! I bet they're going to get a workout tonight.

The engine of her Chevy Volt hummed with more power than any of her non-hybrid driving friends ever expected it to have. She loved her car; it was a good representation of how she felt about life and the responsibility she believed each person had for the future of the planet.

Kyra was well-known to go off on a tangent about society and politics at every given opportunity, and she recognized that owning such a car basically meant going off on a silent tangent each time she drove.

She wasn't confident that it made an impact on anyone else, but it made her feel better to know she was doing her part.

She was meeting her fiancé, Ben, at a restaurant located almost forty minutes away. He'd been at Cabin Green for a few days, having a bachelor party of sorts. Their chosen destination was in his path. It was also one of her favorite restaurants.

Mmmm... I can't wait to eat veggie lasagna.

Ben always wanted to see Kyra as soon as he returned to town from any vacations or work trips, but he was also always excessively tired. She'd grown used to the routine and had learned to enjoy the time they did spend together. She also knew that after he got a good night's sleep, they would have an enjoyable day of getting reacquainted with each other before rushing headlong into the last few days of pre-wedding madness.

She smiled to herself while thinking about the various different ways he would show her how much he'd missed her, and vice versa. Sometimes, she thought his trips were a gift. They gave the couple just enough time apart to truly appreciate each other, and they also kept the sexual spark between them very much alive.

Ben was stunned that he could hear her thoughts while watching all of this from the unforgiving kitchen chair. The one thing no couple had ever been able to experience, but that most had longed for, was this level of intimacy. He was glad to learn how much she'd enjoyed their post-trip visits, and he felt a tremendous sense of loss at having never known any of Kyra's other innermost thoughts.

As difficult as it was to watch her now, he was also as enamored of the sight of her as he'd ever been. This thing that he'd avoided for so long seemed to be equal parts blessing and curse.

Kyra drove on at five miles per hour faster than the posted speed limit, looking forward to the meal almost as much as seeing Ben. *Ha! I bet Ben wouldn't be too happy to hear that.*

Her eyes fell down upon her modest engagement ring, and it warmed her insides to think about the day he'd proposed. Her friends and family thought the two of them were moving forward too quickly when they announced their engagement, but she'd never put much stock in the advice of others. She went with her own instincts and was resolved to deal with the good and the bad that came from this way of living life. So far, she had not been disappointed.

Besides, a year is plenty of time to know someone before proposing. And it's almost been two years now since we met.

Time slipped by as Kyra entertained herself with a mixture of reflection and the occasional outbursts of singing that went along with blaring the radio. She was currently listening to the wedding playlist she'd put together while Ben was out of town, including the song she'd secretly selected for the first dance at their wedding reception. *'Somebody'* by Depeche Mode had been an easy choice because the lyrics accurately depicted their feelings about each other.

Learning this caused Ben to choke out a sob; it was the same song he would have selected if given the choice. They had been so perfectly attuned to each other, even musically. He couldn't imagine living the rest of his life without her if he somehow made it through this nightmare alive.

She was thrilled Ben had given her the playlist duties and had turned everything into the DJ a few days ago. She was also astounded by how much work went into planning a wedding, even one as simplistic as the one they'd be having in about a week. There were several times throughout the planning process when she thought about suggesting scrapping everything and getting married at the courthouse, but she knew her family would be upset.

Kyra was aware how odd it was to plan a wedding more around the guests than the soon to be newlyweds. But she figured it wasn't all that rare of a phenomenon, for how many sane people would follow the hardest route possible if they were the only ones whose feelings were being considered?

The scene changed without warning and Ben saw himself inside of a black rental car, blaring the radio to help keep himself awake. The last few days were a lot of fun, but they'd also left him fatigued. He was overjoyed at the prospect of sleeping in his own bed again.

All weekend, his friends had ribbed him good-naturedly about getting married. Rather than being daunted by this, Ben found himself more determined than ever that life with Kyra made perfect sense. *We're like peanut butter and jelly or macaroni and cheese – made for each other.* Something inside of her spoke to something inside of him in a language no one else could understand.

He couldn't wait to see his beloved and begin the final push to their big day. He also had the next three weeks off work for the wedding and honeymoon, which brought an excited, but exhausted, grin to his face. It was all going to be fantastic, but first he had to make it through dinner.

Kyra had been so excited at the prospect of eating at a specific restaurant along his route that he hadn't had the heart to tell her he would have preferred to grab some takeout and cuddle on the couch. Besides, he would undoubtedly wake up some when he saw her as she'd always had an invigorating effect on him.

He hummed out loud, attempting to keep his mind active. When that failed, Ben rolled down the windows of the rental car and was hit in the face with a refreshingly sharp blast of crisp air. Regrettably, it also brought an unexpectedly huge quantity of rain water with it.

The rain had been falling steadily for the past fifteen minutes or so. The ground in front of him looked sodden with water. He was on one of the most desolate stretches of road within the general area, and it had the misfortune of collecting rain in a way that a newer, better constructed road usually wouldn't.

Kyra turned her car onto the back road with her new windshield wipers flying furiously across the front windshield. They worked perfectly, keeping pace with the water that insistently pelted everything within its path. Her headlights reflected off a large puddle on the road in front of her, and she slowed down a bit to avoid hydroplaning.

Should I call Ben to check on him? He'd been loaned several clunker rental cars in the past, so she always worried about his road trips.

No, talking on the phone would be too much of a distraction.

As she lowered the speed of the Volt to match the road conditions, Kyra thought she heard the distant honking of a horn. It was difficult to make out any specific noises over the roaring of the rain and thunder. She wasn't sure how to react, if any reaction was necessary at all. People in this area had the obnoxious tendency to lay on their horns for no specific reason. When she didn't immediately spot anything wrong, she put the sound out of her mind.

Ben spun around the corner, hydroplaning off one waterlogged spot after another and laying on his horn to warn other drivers he was having difficulty staying in his lane. He didn't see any other cars nearby, but he always thought it was better to be safe than sorry.

The rain continued to make a mess of his windshield. The road in front of him became increasingly difficult to drive on. He missed his Civic in moments like these, but overall, he believed it was smarter to use a rental car when taking long road trips.

There's no good reason to put all that wear and tear on my car.

He had one last turn to go before getting on the road that would lead him to the restaurant. As he approached it, Ben saw another vehicle driving across his path. He hit the brakes and they seized up. "Anti-lock brakes my ass!"

The rental car slid forward, out of his control. He grabbed the steering wheel and attempted to correct his course. Just as he started to get the situation under control, he hit a massive puddle and the car jumped forward several feet.

He honked his horn again, but it was too late; the rental car slammed into the driver's side of the other vehicle. Sparks flew through the rain-soaked air as the metal collided. The other car's door made a sickening crunch as it imploded under the stress of the impact. A woman screamed as glass went flying everywhere, and the two vehicles skidded several hundred feet before coming to a rest against the side of a tree. Ben hit his head against the steering wheel and promptly passed out.

Back in the cabin, he yelled in anguish as he saw for the first time what the accident had been like for Kyra. He witnessed her screaming as glass shards punctured multiple spots on her body. He saw her become aware that he was in the vehicle opposite her. She struggled to remove herself from her seat, frantic to reach her beloved. Her efforts were thwarted when she discovered she was unable to move more than a few inches. A huge chunk of metal had pierced her left side, leaving her bleeding profusely. Terror drowned Ben's body as he was forced to see what it looked like as life ebbed away from the woman he loved.

In the puzzle vision, Ben regained consciousness with a horrible sense of disorientation and pain. He pulled his head off the steering wheel. There were bright, flashing lights all around him and a series of noises he couldn't quite comprehend. A pair of hands reached in and untangled him from the mess that was once a rental car.

"Are you okay?" a random voice asked him.

He tried to respond, but no coherent words came out of his mouth. He was strapped onto a gurney and placed inside of an ambulance. Next to the ambulance was a vehicle belonging to the county morgue. As the ambulance roared away from the scene of the accident, the morgue vehicle headed in the opposite direction at a much more normal pace. The scene faded to black, like it was the end of a movie, and the puzzle pieces became benign once more.

"It was all my fault," Ben cried out, letting his forehead fall to the table as a new wave of mourning passed through his body and mind. He repeated the same phrase multiple times without any interruption, but once he lifted his head again, the ghost decided to speak.

"Was it?"

"Of course, it was," he said, miserable and longing for the final death knell.

"Hmmm... I think we need a second opinion."

Out of the darkness came another form, one that was much lighter and smaller. It walked toward him and put what appeared to be its arms around his shoulders.

"It wasn't your fault," it said with a deep but somehow beautiful voice.

Ben lifted his head up to face the new visitor to the cabin. Could it possibly be who he was thinking? It seemed crazy, but why not? Hadn't everything that had occurred at this cabin been crazy? His thoughts drifted back to several sexual encounters he hadn't realized he'd experienced until now, and it all made sense. But why had she allowed the other ghost to torment him? Was she punishing him?

As if reading his thoughts, Kyra replied with a hint of a chuckle and a gentle tone of kindness, "No one was punishing you. No one aside from yourself, that is. You brought all the misery of the past several weeks onto yourself. You chose not to purchase enough supplies or cigarettes, you chose to break the doorknob so you couldn't leave, you even hammered the windows shut from the outside to make certain you wouldn't be able to escape."

His eyes grew wide as memories of these actions flooded his mind. "What about the bones? The deck of cards? The old man?"

"All delusions. You're exhausted and depressed, my love. And you have to stop blaming yourself," she said with a great amount of patience.

"What about the darkness? And you?"

"I think you know the answer to that." Her form began to shimmer and become less distinct.

He sighed and said, "Yes, I guess I do. But don't go quite yet. Please."

Kyra hesitated, then returned to Ben's side. He slid off the chair and wrapped himself inside of her transparency, lying his head upon her lap. "I'm ready. I want to go with you. Please take me with you." She stroked his stubbly head as he cried himself to sleep.

* * * * *

Kyra's form flickered a few times. All the compassion and love disappeared from her face, leaving her devoid of her humanity. As she disappeared, Ben's unease turned into an even deeper, impenetrable sleep. While he slipped into a sweet dream about his beloved, the cabin noted a major shift in the air. Unable to cry out a warning, Cabin Green sat dormant, although it tried repeatedly to somehow move or make a sound.

Three dark shapes entered the room. The leader emitted a low, disturbing chuckle as the others flanked Ben's sleeping body. Before he could awake or do anything to defend himself, Ben was lifted into the air yet again by the ominous, powerful darkness. His eyes opened groggily, and his close friend, terror, returned with a vengeance.

"Humans are way too easy to break," the leader whispered mirthfully into his ear. "A dash of misfortune, a pinch of emotional exploitation, and a bit of torture is a winning recipe that never fails to produce a tasty treat. Like mother and father, like son, Ben.

By the way, your anti-lock brakes were fine that night. Kyra hasn't been here, either. That's the only thing that *has* been all in your head," it bellowed in a deep, sepulchral tone before continuing sarcastically. "I was so pleased to hear you say you want to stay with me forever, though. Now, this collection is finally complete."

A scream of horror mingled with rage escaped Ben's trembling lips. With his very last breath, he asked one question: "Why?"

"Why not?" the darkness responded.

Ben tried to scream once more, but it was cut short as the darkness swallowed him whole.

CHAPTER FORTY-SIX

16 Years Ago

Ben sat in his room, fingers shoved into his ears and eyes scrunched up in denial of yet another shouting match. The relationship between his parents appeared to be taking another hit, and he hoped it wouldn't be literal this time.

Sara cowered in the corner of the living room, but she defiantly kept her eyes on her husband, Frank. His tall, imposing presence had become twisted through years of anger and abusive behavior.

"Frank..."

"No. Stop. How many times can we go over this, Sara? Get out of here. I can't... I don't want to see you ever again," he spat virulently.

"Let me help you," Sara implored the only man she'd ever loved.

"Help?" The scorn was evident all over Frank's face. "How can you help, Sara?" The pitch and volume of his voice escalated. A dish flew through the air, hitting her in the right kneecap. She gasped in pain as her husband averted his eyes.

"This isn't living, Sara. Now get the fuck out of here!"

Torn between her dogged loyalty and the will to survive, she hesitated at the front door. This hesitation was all he needed to launch another assault. Blows rained down upon her body, giving birth to bruises that would bloom across her midsection. She'd carried the evidence of his malevolence for far too long.

"Take care of Ben," she cried. "And yourself."

Fleeing into the night, she didn't dare look back. If she had, she would've seen the look of torment upon Frank's face as he retained his kneeling position more than ten feet from where she last stood. His hands shook, but the knuckles were clear of any contusions. It had been this way for almost a decade; anger and fear would seep into his mind, followed by hideous whispers that threatened to push him over the brink from barely sane to a world he couldn't explain.

The truth was that no matter what anyone else thought they saw, he'd never laid an angry finger on his wife. Yes, he'd been a participant in regular shouting matches, but the bruises on her body? Those appeared out of thin air.

He also didn't throw the dish that had hit her. It levitated before hurling itself suicide bomber style against the woman he'd sworn to have, hold, protect, and honor. Things like this had become common place, although they somehow never happened that way with any other witnesses to observe them.

For years, Frank thought he'd gone insane, but Sara helped him put the pieces together. As improbable as it seemed, there had to be a supernatural explanation for everything. Of course, no one would ever believe that, which cast him in the role of the abusive, neglectful husband. He'd tried for years to get Sara to go somewhere safe, but she stuck by his side, enduring unspeakable mental and physical torment.

Somehow, the evil that tainted their home never showed any interest in Ben. Yes, Frank had yelled at Ben many times and had also cruelly mocked him. There were even a few instances of abuse that left him hanging his head in shame. The sad truth was most of that came directly from him, and was rationalized through his twisted attempts at keeping his family safe.

Thoughts such as 'how can he protect himself from an evil spirit if he's such a coward?' and 'perhaps the ghost is only pretending not to notice him but has actually been after him all along' often contaminated Frank's mind and left him believing he had no choice but to lash out if he wanted Ben to live. Sara had a different take on it; from her perspective, Frank's actions were being manipulated by a spectral puppet master. Either way, the end result was the same.

The ghost, or whatever the fuck it was, hadn't launched any direct attacks on their son. They had intuited that this wouldn't change as long as Sara left. Her presence riled the spirit up, making it angrier and more prone to fits of violence. When she'd gone on vacation with her sister last year, Frank had been more like his true self than he'd been in a decade. All the fits of rage stopped. As soon as she came back, his mind became invaded once again.

This had led to a plan. Sara would leave and he'd be blamed, but everyone would remain safe. The negative energy had begun dissipating out of the room the moment she left. He hoped she'd be all right and mourned the loss of the life they thought they'd built together, long before this monstrous intrusion tainted everything.

How the hell am I going to explain this to Ben?

* * * * *

The Next Morning

"Good morning, Sara. My name is Dr. Patel. Can you tell me why you're here?"

Sara furtively side-eyed the balding man. She'd spent the night terrified that the ghost would end up following her. She was also dealing with the lingering effects of the sedative they'd given her after the police dropped her off.

"I'm not crazy," she whispered.

"No one thinks that, Sara. What I would like to know is how you got all those bruises."

"It's not what it looks like."

"What do you think it looks like?" he asked.

With an audible exhale, Sara said, "My husband didn't do this to me, doctor."

"Then who...?"

"*He* did it."

"Who is he, Sara? If you tell me, the police can take care of it."

Her eyes shot open wide and he saw a flicker of fear before she narrowed them again. "No. No one can help us with this. If I tell you... well... you'll never believe me anyway." She slumped down in the chair, resigned to her fate.

He thinks I'm nuts. And if I tell him the truth, he'll see that as confirmation of his theory. But what am I supposed to do? Oh, Frank. Nothing's been the same since the vacation we took to that ugly green cabin eight years ago.

CHAPTER FORTY-SEVEN

Present Day

Doug reached the cabin during the early morning after driving through much of the night. However, his certainty that Ben was at Cabin Green was shattered as soon as he pulled up the drive. Ben's Honda Civic was nowhere to be seen, and the cabin looked deserted. Still, he'd come all this way and had to make sure. Doug pulled his tall, muscular frame out of his beloved, gas-guzzling pickup truck.

It took a few moments of fumbling, but he found the right key and slipped it easily into the entry door's keyhole. With a quick click, the door stood unlocked. Bracing himself for whatever oddity he might discover, Doug opened the door and crossed the threshold.

There was nothing in the cabin that indicated Ben had been there at any point during the past few weeks. To make sure, he looked through the rooms, out by the dock, and even in the outside garbage can but found absolutely nothing. Any last thread of hope he'd been holding on to disappeared. Disheartened and tired, Doug decided to lie down on the couch to rest his eyes.

Two hours later, he awoke from a deep sleep. Disoriented, he looked around the cabin, half-expecting to see Ben with a 'gotcha!' look on his face. When this didn't happen, he sadly left the cabin and headed into the small town ten minutes away.

He didn't expect any positive results, but Doug still talked to the gas station attendant and the convenience store clerk. Neither of them had seen Ben. Before leaving town altogether, he accidentally bumped into an old man smoking a Marlboro cigarette in the parking lot.

"Excuse me, sir. I'm really sorry," Doug said, with a chagrined tone.

"No worries, fella. In fact, you look like someone who needs to talk. Is everything okay?"

Doug hesitated, but then he plunged into a quick version of the story. At the man's suggestion, he pulled out his phone, logged into Facebook, and showed him a photo of Ben.

"Sorry, I haven't seen him. You know what? Maybe he'll still show up. Yeah, you know what, that makes perfect sense. That garbled voicemail you mentioned was probably his way of telling you he's headed this way, not that he's already here."

Doug found himself nodding along to the old man's growing enthusiasm, although the story didn't quite ring true.

"I know what you should do. You have the key to that cabin, right? And you're one of the owners?"

Doug nodded in reply.

"Great! Why don't you go back there and stay for a few days? Make sure your friend doesn't show up before you make the long drive home. What could it hurt, right? And maybe you'll get a good ending to this trip instead of leaving empty handed. What do you say?"

At first, Doug thought everything the old man was saying was nothing more than uninformed bullshit. *If Ben had been on his way to the cabin when he left the voicemail message, why isn't he there already?* But as the man's hopeful words sank into his mind, Doug found himself growing confident that he was actually on to something.

"You know what? I think I will do that, mister. Thank you for the advice. I'm glad I ran into you."

"Think nothing of it," the old man said, while reaching out his hand. "I'm happy to help. I hope you find your friend."

The two shook hands, then Doug turned away to finish walking to his truck. As soon as his back was turned, the old man's warm, smiling face twisted into a gruesome visage. There was still a smile, but this one was full of malevolence. With a twinkle of joy in his eyes, the man thought, *it's time for a new collection. Let the games begin.* Three shadows followed him as he walked away, even though it was a dreary, cloudy day.

If you enjoyed this book, please leave a review on Amazon and Goodreads. It's much appreciated!

Want to know the truth behind the real-life Cabin Green and the one section of this book that was based on a disturbing real-life incident? Read on for the Author's Note.

Looking for something different to read? Excerpts from a Psychological Thriller, a humorous Paranormal Mystery, and a dark, reimainged Fairy Tale are included after the Author's Note!

AUTHOR'S NOTE

I started the first draft of this book in 2007 while sitting at the dining room table of the real Cabin Green (yes, it really exists, and yes, it's really in Northern Michigan). After I finished, I shoved it in a virtual drawer and didn't look at it again for ten years. The version you've just read has many of the same elements as that first draft, but it also came to life in 2017 in new and unexpected ways after I finally pulled the story out of storage. A revised version was released in January 2019. When I compare the original and revised drafts, I'm happy to say that it was definitely worth the wait.

I hope you enjoyed reading this book. I know it's very heavy at times, but so is the depression and grief that helped inspire its existence. And unfortunately, those are two themes that almost all of us can relate to.

Cabin Green in Real-Life

Cabin Green is virtually identical to the actual cabin and the surrounding area, although there's no island in the lake. I didn't see any ghosts while I was there, but the atmosphere was spooky enough to spark the idea for this Gothic novel. The bald eagle, singing loons, and feisty chipmunk are all real, as is the fireplace grate that looks like a face.

Cabin Green can't be found by GPS. It's truly that remote. If anyone there ever does come across a malevolent spirit, they're going to have a very difficult time getting help. So, let's hope that never happens.

[SPOILER ALERT: Read the book before continuing.]

The cat skull on a silver platter was inspired by a real-life incident that I personally experienced about twenty years ago. I reached inside the lower kitchen cabinet of an apartment I'd just moved into, and there it was: a silver platter, with a cat skull in the middle, surrounded by a circle of white powder. It was, beyond a doubt, one of the most unexpected and freakiest experiences of my life. I never found out how it got there or what its purpose was.

Find Your Next Read!

As a multi-genre author, I've got books with many tones and themes that appeal to a wide range of readers. Therefore, if it turns out that Gothic horror isn't for you – or if you also have diverse taste in books – I invite you to check out my other works.

Flip past the acknowledgements page to get a taste of my Psychological Thrillers, Paranormal Mysteries, and Dark Fairy Tales. All of these books are available in the Kindle format and can be read with Kindle Unlimited.

Obligatory Author Stuff

If you enjoyed this book, please leave a review on Amazon and Goodreads, and don't forget to tell your horror-loving friends about it! Always remember: your book reviews and referrals help authors survive and thrive. Your feedback is always important, and it's always appreciated.

You can reach out to me via social media with any questions or comments:

www.twitter.com/aprilataylor

www.facebook.com/aprilataylorhorror

www.instagram.com/aprilataylorwriter

www.aprilataylor.net

Sign up for my newsletter (www.aprilataylor.net) to learn about new releases. You'll also occasionally receive special deals and free stories!

ACKNOWLEDGEME NTS

Anne – Thank you for standing by my side during countless drafts and endless nights when I couldn't talk about anything else.

Brenda – Thank you for being the first person to read and critique this book back in 2007.

Kristen – As always, thank you for the vital role you've played in helping me be able to speak with my creative voice.

Cabin Green – You might not be haunted, but you're very real. Thank you for providing me with the perfect setting to explore Ben's descent into madness.

CORVO HOLLOWS

A Psychological Thriller

Excerpt

Chapter One

An unseen woman's ragged screams had just split the air inside Anna's apartment. She hesitated imperceptibly before jumping to her feet. Without a single thought for her own safety, the tall brunette threw the front door open and peered outside.

The harsh July sun beat down on the pavement and reflected off the neighbor's wind chimes. Sun spots obscured Anna's vision, and she lifted her hand to her eyes in a bid to wipe away the visual disturbances.

Her sight started to clear just as the disorienting and terrifying screams returned. A middle-aged woman with ratty hair, disheveled clothing, and bare feet reached toward her from about one-hundred feet away. Anna's eyes fell first to the woman's bloody feet. Then she spotted a black pickup truck and its elderly male driver. His long gray hair threatened to fly free of his head as he sprung out of the newly parked vehicle.

The woman rapidly advanced upon Anna's doorstep before stopping unexpectedly. Her body shook with the force of her recent exertions, and she appeared poised to scream yet again.

"What's wrong? Do you need help? I can call the police," Anna said in a jumbled mess.

The woman's eyes darted from Anna to the front door. She took a deep breath and said, "Yes, I need help! Please, let me in!"

All of Anna's instincts screamed as she patted her pockets in search of her phone. *Dammit*, she thought. Her phone was nestled safely inside the apartment.

A quick scan of the environment showed Anna that the mysterious man hadn't come any closer. In fact, he stood calmly on the side of the truck and appeared to be watching them with interest. Anna made eye contact with him, and it sent a shiver down her spine.

Something isn't right.

"Look, I'm going to call the police for you, okay?"

"But I already called them. They're on their way," the woman pouted.

"I'm going to call again, just to make sure. Stay there," Anna said while motioning for the woman to remain at her current position, approximately twenty feet away.

A strange smile flitted across the woman's lips, and it accentuated the wrinkles around her mouth. She took one step forward, then another.

"Please stay there," Anna said as sweat trickled down her back and her mind exploded with anxiety.

"This is public property, ma'am," the woman responded while taking two more steps. "I have a right to be here."

Anna's sense of unease officially ballooned into an overwhelming tide of panic. Unsure what to do, she risked turning her back on the woman long enough to re-enter her apartment. That was the plan, anyway. With one firm pull, followed by three successive tugs, she was met by the sickening realization that her screen door had somehow jammed shut.

Stay calm, stay calm. Don't show fear.

Anna glanced over her shoulder and found the woman five feet away, her face transformed by the lupine features of an alpha animal on the prowl. The man stood a few feet closer too, and his hard stare belied his attempt at casual indifference.

It's now or never.

One last, victorious tug broke the door free of its humidity-induced prison. She tumbled gracelessly through the entrance and slammed the door in the woman's face.

Each lock clicked into place as Anna placed her back to the door and slid to her knees. Her breathing raged out of control; hyperventilation had become a foregone conclusion, so she steered into the skid and allowed it to happen.

A few minutes later, she composed herself enough to grab her phone. As her fingers danced across the keypad, she slowly pulled apart two slats in the mini blinds. No one was there, nor was there any sign of the black truck.

"911. What's your emergency?"

* * * * *

Detective Brodsky stood uncomfortably in his suit. Although it was eight o'clock in the evening, the heat index still hovered around one-hundred degrees Fahrenheit. He'd already had a long, arduous day of dealing with an unusual - and still unsolved - murder, not to mention the steady stream of overwrought residents who apparently believed 911 was their personal hotline for airing grievances.

The woman sitting in front of him hadn't deviated from her story during three retellings. He could also sense her fear; it had been more than an hour since the alleged incident, but the tension in the air was still palpable. Although he and his partner, Detective Jones, hadn't found any corroborating evidence, they also had no reason not to believe her story, especially in light of recent local events.

"Okay, ma'am, we're going to file a report, and we'll have a cruiser ride through here a few times a day for the next week or so. It sounds like they were attempting a burglary, so be sure to lock your house and car doors. And let us know if you see them again," Brodsky said while handing Anna an off-white business card.

She looked at it thoughtfully, as if it alone could somehow protect her. "Are you sure it's safe to be here, officer? Should I go to a hotel or something instead?"

"You should definitely do what makes you feel comfortable, ma'am. But in my experience, perps like this don't often return to the scene of their failed attempt. You're on guard now, and they know that. They also know you probably called the police. No, it's much easier for them to go elsewhere."

Unfortunately, he thought. He didn't want anything to happen to her, of course. He just wished that for once criminals would make his life less complicated. After all, if they kept trying to commit crimes in the same places, his job would be a breeze. He could issue as many platitudes as needed to make people like Anna feel better, but truth be told, the burglars she encountered would almost certainly skip town and slip through the cracks. Again.

"Okay," she responded.

He could practically see the cogs spinning in her brain. It was clear she wouldn't be getting much sleep tonight. He decided to take one last stab at calming her down.

"You did the right thing, ma'am. You've got good instincts. I tell you what, if you think you hear or see something out of the ordinary, call us. Anytime, day or night. Dispatch will patch you through to the closest officer if I'm not on duty."

"Oh, but I don't want to trouble you for nothing..."

"It's no trouble, ma'am. Seriously. This is what we're here for."

"Thanks," she said shyly as the officers started making their way toward the door.

"He's right, ma'am," Jones said while exiting the house. "Always listen to your instincts. Have a good night."

The two detectives waited until they were back in their unmarked car to share their true feelings.

"Do you really think it was a burglar?" Jones asked.

"Probably," Brodsky replied.

"Then why did dispatch patch the call through to homicide?"

"Aside from the department being ridiculously understaffed right now?" Brodsky pushed his hair back from his forehead. "I'd say they thought this might be connected to the killer from earlier. And maybe they're right."

Read the rest of *Corvo Hollows: A Psychological Thriller* now! Order your copy from Amazon or Barnes & Noble.

MISSING IN MICHIGAN

Alexa Bentley Paranormal Mysteries Book One

Excerpt

Chapter One

My name is Alexa Bentley, but you can call me Alex. I'm also what you might call a ghost therapist. Think that sounds like a bunch of woo? I did too, until I didn't.

Do you believe all our cares simply melt away and our soul soars weightless after death? I hate to break it to you, but everyone you've ever loved and lost still has all the same baggage. And in some cases, dying makes it even worse.

The hardest part for me is when they don't know their life is over. Imagine having to tell a powerfully psychotic killer that he's dead. Or how about telling a devoted mother she can no longer help her children? It gets messy. And when things get messy in the spirit world, humans often pay a steep price.

That brings us to today. There's a good reason I'm lying flat on my ass in the dusty attic of an old Victorian home in Baltimore. The ghost I'm currently trying to counsel is *not* taking it well.

I steel myself against the inevitable next assault and raise my head. "I'm very sorry for your loss. But you're scaring your wife. Is that really what you want?"

The ghost's cold eyes consider me. Spirits don't look like people envision, at least not to me. Where you might see nothing at all or just the slightest wisp of a darkened outline, I see them as they once were. But even the kindest, most gregarious ghosts often become a hardened version of their former selves. Unfortunately for me, there's nothing kind about this one.

A blast of air engulfs my body as a roar of anguish escapes his spectral lips. I end up on my back again. I've picked more splinters out of my behind than any one person should ever have occasion to, and I'm pretty sure the one that just wedged itself into my skin won't be the last of the day.

Hostility oozes out of him. I do a quick mental checklist. His name is Ronald Bellhouse. He was an accountant. His wife, Maryann, still lives in this house. Well, she did, anyway. His frequent moaning and thrashing have her so afraid that she recently jumped out a second-story window. I guess it's more accurate to say she currently lives at Baltimore General Hospital.

"Maryann needs you to stop this, Ronald. And I'm here to help."

His cruel laughter fills the room. "Help? How could you possibly help me? You're a mortal," he sneers.

"So, you know what you are, then?"

"I'm a god!"

Oh boy. That's not good. Usually they're broken-hearted about being dead, but this one is suffering from delusions of grandeur.

"Okay. Tell me, Ronald... I mean, 'god,' why you're staying in this attic, then. I mean, surely there's much more for you to see, and oversee, in the rest of the world, right?"

He looks me up and down. I can see his non-existent brain doing summersaults. I've clearly given him something new to think about.

"Unless you leave this attic, no one will know they should worship you. No one will know to be afraid of you, either."

He chuckles maliciously. "Maryann knows."

"Sure, but is that really enough? A god like yourself deserves praise and fear from millions, right?"

His eyes light up greedily. "Millions?"

"Yes. You can have it all, but only if you leave this house."

The last hint of hesitation falls away. He flies straight toward me, and I barely manage to hit the deck in time. Great. Another splinter.

As his spirit splits free of the attic where he'd become stuck, his form dissipates. "No!" he calls as he realizes the truth. Leaving the attic means leaving the human realm forever.

I stand up and dust myself off. I'll need to head to the bathroom with my trusty tweezers soon - which I keep on me at all times - but for now, I allow myself to smile at another job well-done. Maryann can come home.

Read the rest of *Missing in Michigan* now! Order your copy from Amazon or Barnes & Noble.

VASILISA THE TERRIBLE: A BABA YAGA STORY

Midnight Myths and Fairy Tales

Book One

Excerpt

Prologue

An embittered, elderly woman surveyed her dilapidated surroundings and meager possessions. A tear formed in the corner of her eye, but it wasn't one of sadness or regret. She had been bested by a young, blonde-haired girl with a trickster's mind and a devil's heart. Of course, no one believed her that day on the hill. But one day they would. She'd make sure of it.

Chapter One

TWO MONTHS AGO

Baba Yaga whistled a happy, off-key tune as she swept her living room. It was a humble home, but she'd always taken great pride in maintaining a level of cleanliness that most people in the village were unable to match. When asked how or why she did it, she always responded the same way: "Cleanliness is next to Godliness."

She knew many of her fellow villagers regarded her with some suspicion because she'd never been married. She understood what society's expectations were, but marriage was the absolute last thing she wanted. Still, her kind, friendly nature and cleanly ways helped her maintain a tenuous hold on her position in the village.

Things had recently taken a turn for the worse, though, and she couldn't quite figure out what to do. Therefore, she resolved to do nothing out of the ordinary. These were perilous times for women of her low stature. She'd even heard ghastly tales of other spinsters being burned at the stake in villages in the New World. Her body shuddered as she considered these stories.

That can't be true. Right?

Lost in such thoughts, she failed to notice the first cries for help that emanated from the edge of the nearby woods. But as the crowd outside grew, it became impossible to keep focusing on her housework.

What has that insufferable brat done now?

The villagers might have given Baba Yaga cautious looks, but she knew who the real troublemaker was – Vasilisa. The young girl had bewitched the entire community, but her lyrical voice and beautiful smile engaged people in a way that made it impossible for them to accuse her of ill deeds.

How they can't see it, I'll never know.

She fumed to herself as she followed the crowd. Sure enough, Vasilisa stood right in the middle of everything.

"And then the witch sprang forth and screamed..."

Baba Yaga turned with a snort and stalked away. Vasilisa's story was obviously fabricated. Witches weren't real, and any civilized person should know that by now. As she glanced back toward the commotion, she recognized the sad fact that everyone else stood enthralled by Vasilisa's story.

The next thing you know they're going to start seeing witches in their hen houses. Ridiculous!

Vasilisa's tale circulated throughout the village, and Baba Yaga soon heard it in its entirety. The girl claimed an evil witch with a long, crooked nose had chased her out of the woods with a broom. Vasilisa also elaborated that the witch shouted a hex at her fleeing back and said, "Watch out, little girl. My sister lives in your village, and she's going to grind you up!"

Baba Yaga made the mistake of voicing her opinion to her neighbor. "That one has quite the imagination, yes?"

The woman's pallor turned a sickly ashen gray, and her jaw clenched in defiance. "Whatever do you mean, Baba? This isn't some fairy tale. There's a real witch in those woods, and there might be another one here in the village. If we don't find and banish her, we're all lost."

The two women stared at each other uncomfortably for a few seconds before Baba Yaga realized the extent of her faux pas. "Of course, yes. Yes. You're right, Maureen. I don't know what I was thinking. It's been a long, hot day, and I feel a bit confused and tired."

Maureen looked her up and down before the hostility began to drain from her eyes. "Oh, Baba. Do you think it's the hex? Come on, let's take you inside. You need to rest. I'll pray with you."

Read the rest of Vasilisa the Terrible: A Baba Yaga Story! This Kindle Short Story is available exclusively from Amazon.

April A. Taylor

Made in United States
North Haven, CT
26 June 2023

38265628R00178